A SKYLARK

FLIES

By Robyn Cotton

A Skylark Flies

Revised edition 2024 is published by Hatherop Books

First edition printed in New Zealand March 2017

Cover design by Betty McCready

ISBN: 978-0-9941330-4-5 (Paperback)

ISBN: 978-0-473-72237-1 (e-PUB)

ISBN: 978-0-473-72238-8 (Kindle)

Disclaimer: Although inspired by true events, A Skylark Flies is a work of fiction. Many of the events and all the characters in this novel are fictitious. Any characters based on real people involved in the events that inspired this novel have been altered to protect their identity. Any resemblance to persons living or dead is purely coincidental.

For sales, permission requests or more information, please contact the author through: www.hatheropbooks.wordpress.com

A Skylark Flies is dedicated to all young women who experience terror at the hands of another. I pray this story will inspire courage, determination and forgiveness.

ACKNOWLEDGEMENTS

I am indebted to my best friend and husband Geoff who has always believed in me and encouraged me to fulfil my dreams. This journey has been as much yours as mine.

I also thank my wonderful daughter Lesley and son Matt for their encouragement throughout this writing journey. This novel began as a way of telling you some of my own story.

I am so grateful to my good friends Margaret, Robert, Katherine and Glenys who not only encouraged me but also gave an invaluable critique of the manuscript. Without you, this book would have stayed in the bottom drawer.

And thanks also to my dear friend Claudia for showing me the pitfalls of using an online translator and for giving authenticity to the Deutsch phrases. And to Jeff, who shared his experiences as a London minicab driver.

Thanks to my very talented niece, Liz, who came up with the cover design. The photo was taken moments before the assault that inspired this story and thus has special significance.

My thanks to the New Zealand Writers' College, who provided me with good insight into the craft of creative writing through the Write a Novel course. A special thanks to my mentor Sonny Whitelaw, who was a fantastic teacher providing detailed feedback and guidance. While I am still learning, your tutelage helped me immensely and gave me the encouragement to complete this novel.

I am especially indebted to George Bryant and the crew at Daystar Books, who believed in my manuscript and had the courage to back me. Thanks also to my copyeditor, Iola Goulton, who not only provided a carefully edited manuscript, but in the process has taught me more about the craft.

Finally, I want to acknowledge all my friends and family who have impacted my life and encouraged me along my journey. My life is so much richer for each of you.

Thank you all.

1

New Zealand, 1989

"The issue is with the thoracic cavity. We can remove the first rib to ease the problem." The impassive grey-haired man sat behind his large mahogany desk, his long lean fingers playing with a gold pen.

Rose took her time, uncomfortable under the thoracic surgeon's gaze. It was the worst possible news. She'd thought that a little physio would fix the problem—she hadn't expected this. Dark thoughts threatened and her lip trembled. She drew in her breath and steeled herself. "What does that mean exactly?"

Mr Gurnsey smiled. "We can remove the rib to reduce the distance for the vein and nerve to travel down the arm. Without the operation, there's a good chance you will end up losing your arm. You can see from the colour and swelling that the blood flow is restricted."

"It's not much of a choice, either the rib or the arm." She tried to look upbeat as she concentrated on his words.

"I'm afraid not." His tone was softer. "I can guarantee you won't miss the rib once it's out."

"When will you do it?" Her pulse raced and her hands fidgeted with her rings.

He turned the page of a leather-bound book on the polished desktop and studied it, his brow furrowed in concentration. "If I rearrange my schedule, I could fit you in on Tuesday. It's the earliest I can do and we can't afford to delay it any longer than that." His face took on a paternal look. "You'll need to arrange to take eight weeks off work."

"So soon? And eight weeks off work?" The thought of all she'd need to organise before Tuesday sent her mind into overdrive.

His face was grim as he nodded.

"Is there a downside?"

"I don't expect any complications." His voice sounded confident as he went on to outline the potential risks.

It was almost too much to take in.

"So, I'm confident we'll soon have you fully active and pain-free." He placed his pen down on the notebook. "Any questions?"

"But why? Why now?" It was little more than a whisper.

"I can't say for sure, but it is obvious a severe trauma has caused it."

*

It was late afternoon on an early summer's day when Rose arrived at the private hospital in Hamilton. The calm and sunny day was in stark contrast to the inner turmoil that churned her stomach like the fluttering of a thousand butterflies. She stole a glance at Gary as he drove the car into a park near the austere front door. His strong jaw was set in a grim expression that thinned his lips, making his moustache even more prominent. His fingers tapped a rhythm on the steering wheel. Feeling his tension, she put her hand over his and gave it a gentle squeeze.

She helped the children out of their car seats, careful not to place any strain on her left arm. The shoulder sling made her movements awkward. Lauren's fine blonde ringlets bounced as she scrambled down from her seat and onto the asphalt. Toddler Michael rewarded Rose with his cherubic smile as she lifted him out with her good arm. Now free from his car seat restraints, he squirmed as she hugged him to her. A shrill flute-like warble caught her attention and she glimpsed the trademark white bib and iridescent sheen of a tui sitting high up in a tree. She paused to absorb its beautiful clear melody. As though breathing its song deeply into her soul, she allowed its strength and beauty to resonate, leaving her with a sense of peace that promised hope.

"Mummy, are we at the hospital?" Lauren asked, her blue eyes wide as she looked around.

"Yes, honey, this is it. This'll be Mummy's home for a few days while the doctors and nurses fix me up."

"Are you going to be okay?" Lauren looked up at her with tears forming.

Seeing her edginess had affected Lauren, Rose answered in what she hoped was a matter-of-fact tone. "Yes, Mummy is going to be just fine."

Worry lines were etched into Gary's forehead as he opened the boot to fetch her overnight bag before taking Michael from her. Seeing his concern, she caught his eye and forced a smile, grateful for him and hoping to put him at ease.

Rose took Lauren by the hand and walked in through the imposing front entrance. To the left was the reception area, the counter displaying a large vase of pink and white flowers. The top was wooden and beneath it were hessian covered panels, reminding her of school notice boards. She wanted to pin some bright posters on it to liven it up. Behind it sat a bored-looking young woman tapping away at a keyboard. Rose approached the desk, her footsteps loud on the polished floor. It was quiet, not at all like the busy emergency rooms she would normally associate with a hospital.

"Hi, I'm Rose Cobham. I'm here for an operation on my rib."

The woman glanced up from her screen. "Just a minute." After a quick scan of some documents on her desk she said, "Ah yes, here you are. Please take a seat in the waiting room and a nurse will be with you soon to show you to your room."

Rose turned to lead Lauren and Gary, still holding Michael, placed his arm around Rose's shoulder. Together they walked across to take a seat in the waiting room. A young couple sat huddled together, talking in hushed voices. Their tense looks mirrored how she felt and they acknowledged her polite smile before continuing their conversation. She wondered what they were here for.

A nurse appeared in the waiting room. "Jason Smart?" The young couple got up and followed the nurse up the corridor.

It would soon be her turn. Maintaining her outward calm, Rose surveyed her surroundings. They lacked any sign of home comforts. The waiting room was a small alcove lined with a row of uninviting hard plastic green chairs and a pint-sized table in the corner with a stack of magazines.

On the floor beside the table was a wicker basket overflowing with colourful toys. Lauren made a beeline for the basket and was immediately engrossed in pulling the toys out one by one, spreading them around the floor. Today she looked particularly pretty in a red dress with smocking, a change from the track pants and tees she preferred to wear. Gary put Michael down and, laughing his infectious giggle, Michael scampered on all fours across to join Lauren and latched onto a small tractor that he pushed along while making the appropriate noises.

Gary sat beside Rose with her good hand in his and gently stroked it. Reassured, she rested her head on his shoulder and watched their kids playing together. How lucky she was to have this amazing family. Gary was more than she'd ever dared to dream—not only her lover and best friend, but also her lifeline. And the kids were pure joy. With them all she had hope and a future. She would get through this for them.

Footsteps broke into her thoughts as a nurse strode towards them.

"Rose Cobham?"

"That's me."

"My name's Lyn and I'll be your nurse this afternoon."

"Lauren, how about you pack the toys away so we can go and see Mummy's new room?" Gary asked.

Lauren was never one to miss out on anything and she picked up an armful of toys and threw them back into the basket.

Grinning, the nurse waited until the toys were all away. "This way," she said, and turned on her heel to walk back up the corridor.

Here goes. Rose reached for Lauren's hand and followed the nurse, leaving Gary to follow with Michael and her bag. They passed a number of rooms before entering a sterile cell that had a single bed turned back a little too neatly to be truly welcoming. It was hard to remain upbeat as she took in the stark decor and the window that looked out onto a drab concrete wall. The curtains were a hideous green with orange flowers. As unfamiliar as it was, she'd need to make the most of it because she'd be here at least a week.

I can do this.

"Please unpack your things and make yourself at home," Lyn said.

"Sure." *Home? Really?*

"You can use the wardrobe and drawers." Lyn indicated the small bedside cabinet and the wardrobe next to it, before pointing to the door in the corner. "There's a bathroom in there."

Rose looked at Gary. "This is better than expected. I can't believe I get an en-suite."

"You can get into your pyjamas or nightie if you like. Use this button to call me if you need anything." Lyn indicated a large white button above the bed. "I'll bring you the menu so you can choose your meals. Do you have any questions?"

"No. Thanks."

"Then I'll leave you to get settled in." Lyn's face lit up with a generous smile and she disappeared out the door.

Gary set the bag down. "Just try and relax."

"Don't tell me to relax." He was hovering, which he always did when he was worried. She didn't mean to snap at him, but sympathy only weakened her resolve and she didn't want that. "Look, I'm sorry. This whole situation is making me cranky."

Unpacking would calm her. She laid her nightie on the bed and then placed the toilet bag in the top drawer. One by one she took each item out of her bag and carefully laid them in the set of drawers, then placed the empty bag in the wardrobe. These simple actions distracted her, allowing the crack in her armour to close, until she was once again wearing her brave face.

"Are you going to be alright?" Gary asked as Michael began to squirm and grizzle in his arms.

"Of course. You head home and get the kids their dinner. I'll see you tomorrow after the op."

"Are you sure?" Gary frowned and held her gaze.

She nodded, knowing he wouldn't doubt her resilience. History had taught them that she could overcome anything, especially with him at her side. He had always been her rock, but right now she needed her own space to keep her emotions on an even keel.

"Are you really sure?" asked Gary. "We can stay a bit longer."

Michael sucked his third and fourth fingers, a sure sign he was tired, and reached out to Rose. She took him in her good arm.

"No, it'll be better this way." She kissed the chubby little hand poking her face, and Michael giggled. "I'm looking forward to getting the use of this arm back, and the sooner I get it over with, the better."

"Okay, just remember I love you and I'm only a phone call away." Gary wrapped them both in a big bear hug and whispered in her ear, "I'll be praying for you."

"I love you too, Mummy," Lauren said.

With tears welling up, Rose handed Michael back to Gary before kneeling down to give Lauren a hug. "I love you too, honey." Standing up, she placed her one good arm around Gary and Michael. "And I love you both. Now go and have a yummy dinner."

With a last round of farewells, Gary and the children left.

Sorry to see them go, she went over to the bed and sat down. The starched sheets and hard mattress felt unfamiliar and not the least bit comforting. What would tomorrow bring? She couldn't remember what the surgeon had told her about the risks and she wished she'd paid more attention. He'd sounded so confident she hadn't even thought to ask the hard questions.

Questions like was it going to be painful? And had he ever slipped and cut through someone's nerve or artery or major vein? Was it possible she could lose the use of her arm for good? Doubts circled and unsettled her.

Of course, if it all worked according to plan, she'd get the full use of her arm back. The last few weeks had been hell—having her arm in a sling left her totally incapacitated. Work had been frustrating as well. As a leftie, she couldn't even write. She was angry that even after everything she'd been through—after all the pain and anguish—she now had to face this operation.

It wasn't fair. It wasn't her fault. Why her?

No, she didn't want to think about it. She'd dealt with all that a long time ago. But a deep foreboding had been building over the past few weeks. She'd tried to ignore it, but it wouldn't go away. For years she'd struggled to protect herself by building up layers of resilience. But what if she had to do it all over again? No. It was time to focus on the positive. Tomorrow, she'd be on the road to recovery.

Lyn popped her head around the corner. "How're you doing?"

"I'm okay—just a little scared about tomorrow. I don't know anyone who's had this op before, and I don't know what to expect." Rose took a deep breath and tried to maintain her calm.

Lyn's expression softened and she came over to the bed. "You'll do fine. What a lovely family you have."

It was just what Rose needed. "Yeah, they're great—I'm lucky to have them."

"How old are your kids?"

"Lauren is three and Michael's one. She's a good little helper and like a second mum to him. I think it's why he's not showing much inclination to walk—he just points or utters a demand and Lauren does all the fetching."

"I imagine that's often the way with young siblings." Lyn pointed to the sling. "Can I take a look at your arm?"

"Sure." Rose slipped it out of the sling.

"It's more swollen and blue than I'd like," Lyn said. "Does it hurt much?"

"I get a lot of pain and tingling sensations down the arm, like I've hit my funny bone. The arm's as good as useless now."

"What does the surgeon say?"

"He says there's a problem in my thoracic cavity causing the nerve and vein to be squeezed. Last week I was sent for dye tests, and the x-ray showed a kink in the vein. He said it's probably the result of old scar tissue and he's going to remove the first rib to shorten the distance for the vein and nerves to travel down the arm."

"Well, you're first up tomorrow, so it won't be long now."

Grinning, Rose said, "That's good. I just hope the surgeon doesn't have a big night."

"Not likely. You'll be okay. How did it happen?"

"It's a long story, but it appears my work activities have exacerbated some old injuries."

"Well, Mr Gurnsey is an excellent surgeon and I'm sure you'll soon regain the full use of that arm," Lyn said.

"So I hear." Trying to be light-hearted, Rose said, "I feel a bit like Adam giving his rib for Eve."

Lyn smiled and retied the sling. "What work do you do?"

"I work in product development in the food industry. I was running some trials for new products—lifting heavy buckets when I put my neck out. And that led to this." Rose gestured at her arm.

"And what does Gary do?"

"He's a house husband."

"Really? Good on him. You don't often hear of men taking on the domestic role."

Rose found herself warming to Lyn and she appreciated her professionalism. Lyn seemed to be doing her best to put Rose at ease.

"That sounds like interesting work. Is it hard not being at home with the kids?"

"Not really. Gary does a great job on the home front and I've always been more focused on my career." Now more relaxed, she smiled warmly at her nurse.

"That's good. Now, is there anything more you need of me before I go?"

"No, thanks. I'm fine. I might just read for a bit."

"Okay, just ring the buzzer if you need anything." With that, Lyn turned and left her alone.

Rose busied herself. She undressed and pulled on her nightie, then folded her clothes and slipped in between the crisp white sheets. The book she'd brought promised to be a good read. Although she tried hard to lose herself in it, the words seemed to dance around the page. After rereading the same paragraph several times, she put the book down. Her watch showed it was nearly six o'clock, so she picked up the remote control from the bedside cabinet and pushed the "on" button. The TV roared into life and she scrambled for the mute button to quieten it. The news was about to start and she settled back into her pillow to watch, hoping this would give her the much-needed diversion—at least for a while.

The music started and the news presenter appeared on screen with the usual flurry of headlines. Then the first story unfolded. It was of a young British backpacker murdered while walking on a scenic track in the Bay of Plenty. A picture of a pretty smiling face framed with curly dark hair, flashed onto the screen.

"The victim was touring New Zealand when the senseless attack occurred," the presenter said.

Every hair on the back of Rose's neck stood on end and her skin tingled. The beat of her heart pounded in her ears and her hands became clammy.

The picture switched to a young reporter on location. "The body was found lying beside a popular tourist track." The camera showed a makeshift tent in a cordoned-off area, then panned around the scenic panorama.

"The victim had been taking an early morning hike up the track to take advantage of the scenery when she was violently assaulted and strangled. She was found this morning by a jogger just off the main walking track and beside a rock. As yet, there is no apparent motive for the crime," the reporter said. "Inspector Orr of Tauranga Police is in charge of the investigation."

The camera zoomed out to reveal a man in police uniform and the reporter put the microphone towards him. "The prime suspect, a Caucasian male in his early twenties, has been apprehended and is being questioned by the police. Furthermore, we are not looking for anyone else in connection with the murder."

As the bulletin continued and the reporter told of the shock to the other tourists staying at the same backpacker hostel and to her family in England, Rose shook. Tears welled up and overflowed in a flood, running down Rose's cheeks and dripping onto her nightie. She sobbed with uncontrolled grief. As she absorbed the news item, the stoic wall that she had so painstakingly built up evaporated like steam on a bathroom mirror. The icy chill of terror seized her with its vice-like grip, paralysing her perspective once more. Her pulse pounded. Her hair prickled from the top of her head down her spine. Her skin became damp with sweat.

That poor girl, her last moments must have been horrific. What a tragic way for her life to end. Rose shut her eyes firmly to try and halt the tears, but it was futile. *How terrible for the family. How would they cope?* She wiped fresh tears away with the back of her hand. *It could've been my family!*

The tears just wouldn't stop. And sobs followed, bursting out if she was drowning in emotion.

How ironic the timing was, when she was facing her operation the very next morning.

From the depths of her despair she sensed someone slip quietly into the room. Lyn sat down on the bed beside her and gently placed her arm around Rose's shoulders, hushing her tenderly.

"What's the matter?" Lyn passed her the box of tissues.

"I'm s-s-sorry." She blew her nose noisily. "The news on TV brought back a whole lot of memories I thought I'd dealt with. In fact, it's the cause of my problem and the reason I'm here."

The tears continued to flow.

And the memories flooded back.

2

Scotland, 1981

Rose was waiting at the bus stop and would soon be in Grandma's precious Lesmahagow, a tiny village on the edge of moorland near Lanark in the central belt of Scotland. After seven months working in London, she'd finally managed to wrangle time off to escape the city and make her long-anticipated visit. Not only was she named after her grandma, but her mum always said she took after her. But even more than this, her own life felt inextricably linked to that of her grandma's. Family was everything and connecting with her roots was important.

Simply by being here and connecting to her family's past was likely to change her, but how exactly was unclear. For a tree to blossom, it is fed through its roots—she hoped it'd be the same for her.

The eight-hour bus trip had been long and uncomfortable. It was such a relief to stand and stretch. The return ticket had cost fifteen quid, more than half her weekly wage. However, she'd waited her whole life to make this visit and it would be worth every penny. Now she was waiting for Ted, a bachelor and elderly cousin of her mother's, who had offered her a place to stay.

As the crowd thinned, she spied a short stout man of about the right age looking at her. She couldn't be sure it was him—she should've thought to ask him to wear a funny hat or something in his buttonhole.

Stepping towards him, she asked, "Ted?"

"Aye, you must be Rose." He put his hand out and Rose shook it. "Welcome to Scotland."

"Thanks. It's great to be here at last."

"Well, let's be having you then." His voice was gruff as he picked up her bag.

They were soon loaded into a mustard-coloured Ford Escort, and Ted pulled out of the car park. She studied him shyly as he concentrated on the traffic. He looked vaguely familiar, and she racked her brain trying to recall a connection. Then it came. He resembled the captain from *Dad's Army*, with a frown that seemed to stem from his jowls, a bald head lined with a tuft of short silver hair, and the moustache to match. He wore a brown tweed sports jacket with a leather patch on the elbow, and what looked like a homespun jersey and grey trousers. The only thing missing was the spectacles.

"Tell me about yourself, lass. I hear you've been at university," Ted said.

"Yes, I spent the last three years studying science. I'm not sure what I want to do with it yet, but my priority was always to head overseas and visit Scotland before settling down. When I was studying, I worked part-time and saved enough to buy my ticket. Then as soon as I finished, I flew out and managed to score a nanny job in London."

"Well, we're pleased you've come to see us."

"Thanks. I can hardly believe I'm here. I was close to Grandma and spent a lot of time with her when I was growing up."

"Is that right? She left Lesmahagow a long time ago. Never knew her myself."

"She always talked about *our* home in Lesmahagow. When in school, I always said I was part Kiwi, part Scottish. It's kind of like I'm on a pilgrimage home and it's been my dream for as long as I can remember."

"You don't say. That's quite something, I hope we don't disappoint." Ted chuckled. "You'll find Lesmahagow fairly typical of these parts. Even though the population is in the thousands, we still think of ourselves as a village."

"Oh, I'm sure I'll love it. I can't imagine the wrench it must have been for Grandma to leave the home she loved and sail halfway across the world."

They drove on in silence for a few minutes. "How was London?" Ted asked.

"Good ... and big. I'm a live-in nanny for a Jewish family, the Cohens, in North London. They're lovely. Do you know London at all, Ted?"

"Nay, not well, lass."

"We live in Totteridge, a really charming suburb with lots of trees and we even have access to a private lake. The houses are all mansions with large gardens. The Cohens treat me well, although I do miss home. But the work's easy, which is a nice change after uni. I really love looking after their little boy Daniel, who's just three. I didn't plan to be there so long—it's been seven months already—but I've decided to stay on for another month to see the royal wedding." Talking about herself was helping her relax.

"Aye, lass. That's going to be quite a show," Ted said.

"It sure will. The newspapers and magazines can't seem to get enough of them. I'm lucky it's all happening while I'm here."

"Was it hard finding work there?"

"No, not really—I applied through an agency. The nanny agency is pretty much run by the owner's nanny, Stephanie, who's Australian. She organises us girls to meet socially and there's quite a group of us who hang out together on our days off, from all different countries. It's heaps of fun."

"That's good, lass. Best not be lonely."

"No chance of that. I'm planning to trip around Europe in a couple of months with Kathy, one of the girls." She paused. "What about you, Ted. What did you do?"

"I'm retired now, lass, from the army. Spent most of my life stationed in India."

She stifled a giggle knowing she'd nailed it—he really did look like the quintessential army major. And she wondered what came first, the stereotype or the man?

"Like a good curry then?" she asked.

"Aye, lass—the hotter, the better."

They lapsed into awkward silence.

"We're almost there, lass," Ted said at last. "See those turrets over there among the trees? That's Birkwood Castle, a gothic mansion."

Rose thought it looked eerie.

As they entered the village of Lesmahagow, she was struck by the rows of identical terraced houses and a distinct lack of colour. She was a little disappointed, even though she wasn't sure what she'd expected. The brown, stony-grey, beige and off-white seemed dull and depressing—and it didn't help that the day was dismal and grey.

They pulled up outside Ted's place, a small but neat bungalow on the hillside. He insisted on taking her bag and she followed him inside.

"Welcome to my wee place, lass. I'll be showing you your room then, so you can freshen up if you want."

He led her through the kitchen and into a hallway, pointing out the bathroom before entering a single bedroom where he put down the bag. The house was as neat on the inside as it was on the outside—a fitting home for a bachelor who'd lived under army discipline.

Later that day, a number of Ted's siblings and their families called around, no doubt curious to meet their foreign cousin. They filled the cosy sitting room with noisy chatter and the gathering soon turned into an impromptu party, fuelled by homemade carrot whisky and dock weed wine. Rose was at ease, enjoying the warmth shown to her—it was almost as though she'd known them all her life. She took a liking to Andy, one of Ted's nephews, who was around her age. He had a muscular build with a ruddy face that smiled a lot and he teased her in a thick Scottish brogue, although she was sure he was putting it on because none of the others were half as difficult to understand. After the last of the revellers left, she sank into her bed exhausted but happy.

*

Next morning, she was sitting in the lounge loading a film into her camera when Ted walked in and passed her a cup of tea. Although outwardly awkward, he seemed to be doing his best to make her feel at home.

"I believe your Grandma, Elspeth, was my mother's youngest surviving sister. They were a large family, fourteen in all, although only eleven survived infancy—that was fairly common back then."

Rose grinned. "I couldn't imagine being part of such a big family."

"Ach, it was before TV of course." Ted chuckled at his joke.

"I think Grandma Elspeth was one of the younger ones, born in 1896 to Great-grandfather's first wife."

"Aye, lass, I have the family Bible over there. We can check that out if you like." Ted removed a large, thick book from the bookcase and passed it to Rose, who fingered it apprehensively as if she were touching the fingerprints of her ancestors, as if the book somehow connected her to her history, her roots. The dark brown embossed leather was scratched and curled at the corners from decades of use. Inside, family births, deaths and marriages were neatly inscribed. Handling it carefully, she flicked through the thin pages before handing it back.

Ted opened the front cover. "Here it is—your Grandmother Elspeth was the tenth child. Agnes, her mother, was the first wife who bore twelve of his children before tragically dying in childbirth. It looks like your grandma would have only been two and a half years old."

"Grandma said her sister Maggie pretty much raised her."

"Aye, she did, until she was married. Ah, here it is, Maggie was the eldest and would've been eighteen years older than Elspeth. She emigrated to New Zealand after she was married, but you'd know all that."

"Grandma was very fond of Maggie. I gather she was like a second mother."

"The old man must have been desperate for help with his extensive family because he married twice more." Ted paused to consult the Bible before continuing. "By my calculations, Elspeth would have been just seven years of age when Maggie moved out. And she would've been nine when the old man married his second wife, a sickly woman by all accounts, who died only three months after the wedding. The old man caused a stir when he married the housekeeper just two years later. My mother always said it was a marriage of convenience. This woman came with an illegitimate son and then she had one more child to your great-grandfather."

"He didn't seem to have any difficulty in attracting a wife." Rose paused and studied Ted. "Do you think Great-grandfather could have been the father?"

"Nay lass, I should think not. And wives apparently came easy to him." Ted afforded another chuckle. "Perhaps because he was considered an upstanding man in the parish. Or maybe it was his boot shop? Back in the day, a man who could provide a comfortable home and enough food would probably have been considered a good catch—enough to keep them out of the workhouse."

"That's understandable," Rose said. "Can you tell me more about Lesmahagow? What's its claim to fame?"

"Well now, let me see. It's been here a long time. They recently found pottery dating back to the Stone Age." Ted paused as he took a sip of tea.

"Wow, that's impressive." Taking a moment to consider this, she added, "The Māori didn't settle New Zealand until around the fourteenth century, although some say there were an earlier people inhabiting its shores when they arrived."

"It's a young country you have there."

"What do people do for work around here?"

"Ach, there's a lot of unemployment around these parts now, lass. We were thriving once with the coal mining just down the road at Coalburn. There used to be a real demand for the coal, but that's all changed." Ted frowned. "Now the demand has dropped right off and we've been hit with mass redundancies. The railway line that runs through the village is now a disused monument to remind us of those better times."

"Sorry to hear that. Unemployment brings all sorts of issues."

"Aye, it's a problem for the youth in the village, that's for sure. Some of the local lads don't seem to do anything except sit around drinking and causing trouble. Others have left in droves to find work in the cities. Scotland has significantly higher unemployment than the rest of the UK." Ted sighed and took a long drink before continuing. "Maggie Thatcher has a lot to answer for. She hasn't been kind to this region. The losers under her policies are Scots, young people and the unemployed."

"So what needs to change?" She looked quizzically at him then picked up her cup and drained the last mouthful. Tea leaves lined the bottom and she remembered how her grandma would place the cup upside down on its saucer, turn it and pretend to read the tea leaves. What would Grandma make of Lesmahagow today?

"Aye, lass, that's the big question. A government sympathetic to Scotland and its social problems would be a good start. But what do I know?"

"We've had an interior decorator, Bill, working on our house. He's been good company. He tells me about Mr Cohen's property development ventures. Apparently he's incredibly rich and owns real estate all over London, but you wouldn't know it living there because they're so down-to-earth. Bill is one of a small band of tradesmen who work full-time on Mr Cohen's properties. He's got some interesting stories about wealthy tenants, Saudi princes and aristocrats' spoilt children. It's a whole different world to the one you're talking about."

"Aye, there's money about. There's a huge contrast between the wealthy and the likes of us up here in the north." Ted stared at his cup as though deep in thought before changing the subject. "Now, lass, are you set for a visit to the boot shop this afternoon? I've asked Jock MacGregor to show you around the old place, not that there's much to see. He's expecting you about two o'clock."

"Absolutely, I'm really looking forward to it. Grandma talked so much about it. She never did get her Lesmahagow home out of her blood."

"Good. You might also like to visit the Abbeygreen Church, where the family went. Your great-grandfather was an elder there, a real stalwart of the congregation and a pillar of the community." Chuckling, Ted added, "My mother said he was a formidable character—very strict, and the household lived and breathed by his rules."

"I'd like that. Grandma said the old minister used to preach about hellfire and brimstone and it scared her half to death."

Ted grinned. "The current one does as well, lass. We get a right tune up each Sunday."

"Grandma said when she was young, fun was forbidden on Sundays. Dancing was her passion, but she wasn't allowed to do it on a Sunday. They couldn't even play with the cigarette cards the family collected. Sundays must have been boring."

"Aye, lass, thankfully times have changed." Ted got up and collected the empty cups. "Well, don't be late for Jock MacGregor—it's kind of him to agree to see you."

*

The boot shop was near the Post Office and towards the end of a row of terraced shops that all had rooms above. The cladding on the building looked old and dull, covered with decades of grime. A large bold sign hung over the window, advertising the treasure trove of shoes that were for sale inside. She couldn't wait to explore.

As Rose opened the door to the boot shop, a small bell strategically placed above it heralded her arrival. Inside there were shelves covered in rows of neatly arranged pairs of shoes. A jolly looking little man stood behind the counter. He had thick grey curly hair and was wearing wire-framed glasses.

"Mr MacGregor?"

"You must be Rose. Ted said you'd like to take a look around. I have to tell you, I don't really use the upstairs anymore, but you're welcome to take a gander."

"Oh, that would be great. Grandma told me so much about the shop and what her life was like here. I'm so excited to be seeing it for myself."

"Well, not a lot has changed down here. I've modernised the display stands and moved the counter here from where it was over there." He pointed across the room. "Your great-grandfather was a very good bootmaker in his day. People came from as far as Hamilton to get their shoes from him. That was a long time ago." He paused before carrying on with what appeared to be an afterthought. "Funny how this old shop has continued selling shoes. Must be meant to be."

Rose walked over to the shelves of women's shoes and picked up an elegant sandal. She tried to imagine the shelves full of styles from Grandma's day.

"You have some nice shoes here."

"Aye, thanks. Look, why don't you come out back and I'll show you the rooms upstairs?"

Eager to explore Grandma's childhood home, Rose followed him around behind the solid old counter, through a door into a small and dingy room. A narrow and rickety wooden stairway with an old wooden banister stood against the back wall. Most of the space in the little room was under the stairs, organised with an assortment of shelves full of boxes and folders. An electric jug sat on one shelf with what looked to be an antique teapot, tea caddy, some cups and jars of condiments. It was possible these had once belonged to her own family.

"This way." Mr MacGregor started up the stairs, which creaked in protest as they strained under his weight. "Mind your footing. The stairs and the rooms above should be condemned. I don't like to go up there too often these days, but as you are a very special visitor, we'll make an exception. Oh, and don't trust the bannister either."

"Okay, thanks. I'll be careful." As she reached the top, she paused to look around and was disappointed as she took in the general decay.

"There are just the two rooms, a bit of a mess I'm afraid. The other room was the bedroom and this was the living area and scullery. There's no bathroom—they would've shared a water closet with the neighbours."

The bell below sounded as someone entered the shop.

"I best be getting back to the shop. You can have a look around. Just be careful and mind your footing when you come back down."

"Thanks so much, Mr MacGregor. It means a lot to me to be able to see this place. I won't be too long."

"Aye lass, take as long as you like." Mr MacGregor turned and disappeared back down the stairs.

The tiny two-room apartment hinted at the cramped squalor the family must have lived in. Two small windows let in a few shafts of daylight, which highlighted an old fireplace covered in a fine grey web. She moved over to an old sink and ran her hands along the cracks and flinched as a cockroach ran out of one. The family had cooked, eaten, cleaned and played in this room. Making boots was an honourable trade, but it obviously didn't make the large family wealthy. No wonder the older ones were encouraged to leave the nest early. They needed to, in order to make room for their younger siblings.

She wandered into the adjacent room, a floorboard creaking as she walked. The room was empty apart from a stack of old cardboard boxes in the corner and a thick covering of dust on the wooden floor. Stories from her childhood began to come to life as she imagined them all sleeping in this room—the siblings topping and tailing in one bed, with a second smaller bed for their parents. She remembered hearing the beds were more like wide wooden shelves with lumpy mattresses and when the family outgrew it, another layer was added. Like trays in an oven. Against the wall was another small fireplace, a necessity in the harsh Scottish winters even with the warm bodies in the bed.

She was beginning to see why her young grandma left.

Rose moved back through to the living room, taking care not to step on the squeaky floorboard. She peered out through the window smeared with decades of grime. On the sill was a wooden instrument that looked like it might be used to stretch shoes. She picked it up and fiddled with the screw. *Grandma, what was your life like?*

When Rose was young, Grandma had filled her head with stories of her own life growing up in Lesmahagow as they dusted the china cabinet or cleaned the silver together. Grandma had always talked fondly of her big sister Maggie, who would shield her from their father's not infrequent harsh punishments. Great-grandfather, believing children should be seen and not heard, would quip, "He that spareth his rod hateth his child, but he that loveth his child chasteneth his child betimes."

Taking in the dilapidated scullery area, she imagined her young grandma scrubbing it clean and perhaps even having to carry the slops downstairs. She could imagine Maggie teaching Grandma Elspeth to sew, helping her to get the stitches small and even. Perhaps Maggie would also help Elspeth with her homework, until the letters were neat and the sums right. Fond memories of her own childhood flooded back as Rose recalled Grandma teaching her to mix and knead scones. Better still was the way Grandma had helped her make biscuits, mixing the dough and rolling it out on the bench so she could cut them into shapes and place them on the trays. Her eyes glistened as she was overwhelmed by her feelings for this extraordinary woman.

Grandma Elspeth must have been devastated when Maggie left to marry Campbell. The stepmothers came into her life, but no-one could have replaced Maggie. She would have barely known her first stepmum before she died. And the housekeeper who became her second stepmum was apparently a hard woman who constantly reprimanded her. How cruel to lose the second most important woman in her life when Maggie and Campbell set off to emigrate to New Zealand. Staring down at the street, Rose could sense how hard it must have been for Grandma to see the carriage take away her precious Maggie. *Grandma, you followed your sister to New Zealand and had your family there, but why did you never call it home?*

Grandma was by nature a fun-loving person and a romantic at heart, who had always loved music and dancing. One New Year's Eve, she'd crossed the knives and danced the sword dance on the table to a room full of revellers. Rose could imagine her here as a young girl, dancing about the living room in an imaginary Scottish reel.

A small wooden table stood in the corner, covered in old papers and posters advertising shoes. As Rose rifled through them, she remembered photographs of her young and attractive grandma, no doubt popular with the boys. Grandma had fallen in love with one of the local lads named Eric, who was determined to find a better life abroad. He left for New Zealand, working his passage as a sailor, but not before he'd popped the question and slipped a ring on her finger.

Grandma had left home to follow him to New Zealand in 1914, making the voyage alone. Stricken with seasickness, she'd spent the miserable one-hundred-day voyage confined to her cabin. Even so, it was her ticket out of the cramped family quarters and into a new adventure. She would have been full of hope for a better life, but she'd never see her father again.

The family in Scotland must have known only a little about New Zealand and the images of what lay ahead were probably based on sporadic letters from Maggie. New Zealand must've seemed a long way from Scotland and everything she had ever known.

Compared to Grandma's, Rose's journey had been a breeze. The flight was comparatively quick, her expectations were realistic thanks to media and pictures. Modern communications were light years ahead—she could call home any time and letters only took a week. And she had a credit card. Even so, she recalled how nervous she'd been, waiting to board the flight in Auckland. London had seemed a long way from home. Grandma had been a brave woman to make her one-way voyage alone, to what was in many respects still a frontier.

For Grandma, hope turned into tragedy when she arrived to discover her fiancé was a drunk. She'd ended the relationship, found a place in a boarding house in Wellington, and took work cleaning houses to make ends meet.

And then along came a handsome young Shetlander called Jock, an engineer aboard a merchant ship based in Wellington. He was a real gentleman and by all accounts adored Grandma. Even so, it seemed like she'd approached this courtship cautiously, because it went on for some years. They'd finally taken the plunge and married in 1921. Although New Zealand was their country of residence, Grandma was proudly Scottish and even after sixty years of living abroad, she'd still spoken with a broad Scottish accent, still called Lesmahagow "home".

A bell rang in the shop below, snapping Rose back to the present. She made her way down the stairs, careful not to fall.

Mr MacGregor looked up from the counter as she re-entered the shop. "How did you get on then?"

"That was amazing—I can almost sense the family living up there. It's helped bring my grandma's stories to life. Thanks so much."

"I'm glad I could help. Enjoy the rest of your stay in Lesmahagow. And if you want to come back and take another look, just let me know."

"Thanks, Mr MacGregor. I will." She beamed before turning and going out through the door, leaving a jangling sound behind.

The weather was unseasonable for June, grey and damp with incessant drizzle. She walked up the street, stories and memories flashing through her mind like a kaleidoscope. She barely noticed the cold as she tried to make sense of them all. Grandma's life here was so different to her own. And this town was unfamiliar and very different to the one where she'd grown up.

Melancholy settled over her like a veil. For the first time, it dawned on her that she had only one home and it was in New Zealand. She loved her home, its colour and space. She loved the spacious housing where an average Kiwi family lived in a bungalow and state housing was provided for the poorer families. She loved the sunshine and warmth in summer, when you could visit a beautiful beach and spend all day without seeing another family. She loved the majestic bush with its native birds, free of snakes and other harmful creatures. Pride rose up as she thought of the unique Kiwi culture, its Māori heritage—and the haka, the stirring warrior dance.

And then there were her mum and dad, her siblings and all her friends—how she missed them all. She was a Kiwi through and through.

And there was Gary. They'd met at a university rugby club cabaret, only six weeks before she left New Zealand, and now she was counting the days until she'd see him again. Sometime during their exciting whirlwind of dates she'd fallen for him and had she not already booked her tickets, she'd have been tempted to stay and wait for him to finish his studies. His mail became the highlight of her weeks, each letter exposing more of his inner thoughts and feelings. She dreamed about being with Gary, of picking up where they'd left off, maybe even getting married and having a family together. New Zealand was where she wanted to live out her life and where she wanted to raise a family.

New Zealand was home.

Perhaps Grandma had never called New Zealand home because she'd related 'home' to where she'd grown up, where her parents were. And like Grandma, Rose's home was where she'd grown up. Not here. Grandma's home was part of her history, but it wasn't Rose's story.

3

Rose woke up to another grey day with the cool north wind blowing its icy air over the Scottish lowlands. So much for summer. Ted was already up cooking a pot of porridge and he handed her a steaming bowl as she came into the kitchen. Grateful, she sat opposite him at the Formica table to eat the warm gruel, finding it surprisingly good.

"What would you like to do today, lass?" he asked as he scooped up another spoonful.

"Well, I'd like to take a photo of the town. Where do you think I should go to get the best view?"

"I suggest you go back down to the village and then take the road called Langdykeside, go over the iron bridge and head up the hill. You'll come to an old railway track, and if you follow that, you should get some nice pictures looking back down over the town."

The idea of exploring excited her and she was eager to finish her breakfast. "That sounds like a plan. Do you want to come?"

"Nay, lass. I'll stay here and tend my garden—this ol' knee doesn't like the hills. There are some interesting excavations at the old abbey you could explore on the way."

They collected their empty plates and chatted some more about the excavations while finishing the dishes.

After helping Ted with a few more household chores, she pulled a borrowed anorak on over her open-neck shirt, cardigan and jeans.

"I'll be off now, Ted," she called out, slinging her bag with the camera inside over her shoulder.

Ted poked his head around the door, "Aye, come back in time for lunch. You'll need that anorak."

"That's for sure. Bye." She put on her walking shoes and ventured outdoors. The cold wind hit like a barrage of icy needles, and she zipped up the anorak.

She loved to play the tourist, exploring new places, and today was no exception. Her mood was upbeat, despite the dismal day. She strolled down the hill from the house, breathing in deeply and filling her lungs with the country air. It felt so good after her time in London. Humming some old Scottish tunes her grandma had taught her, she greeted those she passed with a ready smile while taking in the village sights.

Across the valley and to the east, she could just make out a cut along the green hillside and guessed it was the track Ted was talking about. Beyond that and further up the hill was more of the housing estate. The peacefulness of the village was shattered by the sound of heavy earthworks going on somewhere close by, but even loud noise couldn't ruin her buoyant mood as she enjoyed the morning.

Down Baker's Brae and around the corner, she found herself once more outside her grandma's old boot shop and she paused to take a photo. On a whim, she went down the alleyway beside the shop and surveyed the small area out the back, remembering the stories Grandma told about getting into mischief with her little brother, Johnny. Great-grandfather kept coloured Cocktail cigarettes behind the counter and occasionally she'd help herself to some when he wasn't looking. She must've thought it was grown up to smoke these slimline cigarettes in the long holders. She and little Johnny would sneak out around the back of the shop to smoke them. Grinning, Rose wondered if maybe this was hereditary, given her own early smoking antics.

Backtracking out from the alleyway, she found the priory excavations and strolled about the mounds of earth and scattered stone. The sign said it was founded in 1144 by Benedictine monks and she wondered what it would have been like to live in medieval times. Hungry for history, she pulled out her camera and snapped some photos.

Moving on, she crossed the Old Parish Church yard and walked up Langdykeside onto the path to the iron bridge. Pausing, she leaned on the rail and imagined how Grandma might have played around here with Johnny. The sight of the flowering lilac shrubs on the hillside reminded her of the sprig of pressed heather Grandma had kept in her Bible. Had this been one of Grandma's favourite places? She could picture Elspeth running and dancing about the meadow, tumbling on the heather and letting it cushion her, tickling her bare skin. Maybe she had come here to dream of being free. Maybe even dreaming of sailing the world one day.

The path took Rose up the hill and onto a track that was a forgotten railway line. Although it was covered in long grass and the iron tracks and sleepers had been removed, she could still feel the rough ballast rocks underfoot. The feel was familiar, reminding her of the times playing around the railway line near where she'd grown up. The track hugged the hillside, which climbed steeply on one side and dropped away into the valley on the other where the main street ran, and the noise of heavy machinery persisted. The track was green and leafy, bordered with shrubs and yellow flowering gorse, reminding her of home.

She followed the track until she came to a clearing where she could get a good view of the village. The Old Parish Church dominated the scene with its tall spire breaking the grey horizon. The buildings looked drab in the low light, almost lost to the green of the fields and hills. Although it didn't have the ingredients for a prize-winning composition, she needed a keepsake of this special place.

She pulled her camera out of its pouch, flicking it on before sizing up the picture. Satisfied, she snapped the photo, turned it off and forced it into the case.

A noise, barely audible above the din of the earthworks below, startled her and she glanced behind her to see a man walking towards her along the path. She turned her attention back to her camera, only to find herself face down in the grass.

Stunned, it took a moment to work out what was happening. Someone was on her back, pinning her down. Her head seemed to explode as something hit her.

Hard.

And there was another blow. Pain shot through her. Then a noise that sounded like rock against rock.

She wriggled to try and break free but didn't have the strength to move out from under his weight. A rough hand covered her mouth, preventing her from shouting. She tried to pull his hand from her mouth, but his other hand went to her throat and gripped her neck. Tight.

He was strangling her.

It was as if time stood still as the world momentarily stopped spinning. Even the crickets held their breath.

Is this it? Is this how I'm going to die? Here, of all places?

She tried to resist.

How will Mum and Dad cope? What about Gary?

She struggled again in vain.

I don't want to die. Not yet. Not here. I'm too young. I have too much to live for.

She tried again but was trapped under him.

Get off me!

She had no idea how long she was there on the grass, but she had to fight like she'd never fought before. Adrenaline surged, she writhed, she twisted. Over her shoulder she could see his face. His eyes were wide open, vacant, staring. His pupils looked small—like he wasn't really seeing her.

If I poke my fingers into his eyes, will I get away or make it worse?

Instinctively she knew it would make him more frenzied. Then he might really finish her off. She twisted again, desperate to get his hands off her mouth and off her throat.

She needed help. Needed someone to come to her rescue. Using all her strength she managed to get his hand off her mouth for long enough to scream. But he tightened his grip and then the futility of her action dawned on her— the noise of the earthworks at the bottom of the hill would drown out her screams.

No one will come.

She willed herself on. Frantic, she clawed at the hand on her mouth. Tried to scream. She needed air.

A strange lethargy crept over her, dulling her resistance, dulling her resolve to fight, dulling her senses. It felt as if she was floating out of her body. It would be so easy to give in. To just go with the flow.

No. She couldn't afford to lose consciousness. She had to focus. Again she tried to fight and wriggle free, but her strength seemed to ebb away.

So, this is it. This is the end.

She was desperate for oxygen. With one last burst of adrenalin-fuelled exertion, she tried again to get his hand off her throat, making muffled noises through his fingers. She looked over her shoulder and into his eyes, imploring him to stop.

His grip relaxed a little. "If you stop trying to scream, I'll let you go for a minute."

As she looked over her shoulder, she could see his eyes change as he appeared to focus.

She nodded. His hands further loosened their grip and she found her voice. "Okay, I promise." Her voice was broken, raspy.

"If you scream, I'll finish you off." His words were more a growl. But he let go of her neck and slowly got off her back.

She struggled into a sitting position. Hurting all over, she put her hand up to her mouth and realised she was bleeding. She looked down and saw blood on her clothes. That explained the warm sensation.

Get him talking.

Talking. Talking would calm him down while she waited for an opportunity to escape.

"W-what do you want? I've no money on me, but you can take my camera."

No response. Just vacant eyes. Staring. Silence.

"What's the matter?" she asked.

Nothing.

She tried again. "D-do you have a problem? Do you want to talk about it? I'm a good listener and maybe I can help you." It came out a little too fast.

He continued to stare at her.

"Look, you can't just go around doing this to people. You could've killed me." She was beginning to find her courage.

And still nothing.

Then, as though waking from a trance, he spoke, his voice heavily accented. "I don't know what happened."

Nodding slowly, she willed him on.

He seemed to gain confidence. "I don't remember coming across you on the track. I don't remember anything until just now, when you started speaking."

"What's the matter? Do you have a problem?"

"I-I don't know. Ach it-it's all a mess. You don't want ta hear."

"Try me."

"There's a wee baby, my baby. B-but I haven't seen him. They won't let me." He was watching her closely.

"Oh." It was all she could manage. At least he was talking. With effort, she added, "Why don't you tell me about it."

She got to her feet, gingerly, slowly, painfully, ready to seize the first opportunity to escape.

He followed and stood to face her. Close. "Her parents won't let me near him, near them. They've convinced Chrissie, his mum and my girl, to stay home with them. But I'm his Da—I have to see him. And Chrissie's my girl."

Now, how can I escape? The heavy earth-moving machinery seemed to take on a more urgent whine. *There's no point in screaming.*

He continued. "Ach, it's hopeless. They don't like me. They've told her no' to have anything more to do with me. She can't even contact me. They live in London—they're a bit posh."

She nodded.

If I make a run for it now, he'll catch me before I reach the village. He looks fit and the last thing I want to do is to make him mad again. Her best chance was to keep him talking to try and calm him down. And then reason with him.

"Ach, I've nothing to offer." He looked defeated. "No money. No job. No future. I was an able seaman in the Royal Navy. There's no work round here, not without a proper trade behind you. Cripes, I've been unemployed for four years now."

She studied him as he talked, not wanting to forget what he looked like. He was about her height, probably around five foot ten inches and of a wiry, muscular build. Not particularly good looking, with eyes that were speckled brown and dark hair cut short in a skinhead style. There were no notable facial features or anything else that particularly distinguished him. He wore a worn and faded denim jacket over a dark green jersey. His faded jeans had a cuff folded over his work boots, which were old and scuffed.

There appeared to be a packet of cigarettes in the pocket of his jacket.

"I have to talk to Chrissie—I just have to. I want to see them, to patch things up. I need to see my son and to hold him. Curse them all!" His voice sounded more desperate.

Now what? She had to calm him. "You're right to want to see your son." She tried to make her voice sound calm and sympathetic.

"I miss her—I just can't stop thinking about them." His voice was quiet again.

As she listened to him, her own pain diminished as she was drawn into his story, into the hopelessness of his situation. His life was a mess, and she'd become connected to his suffering when their stories had collided. And now, even after what he'd just tried to do to her, she empathised with him.

She wanted to help.

"I wrote her a letter."

"Is that where you were going? To the Post Office?"

He nodded, took a letter out of his pocket and handed it to her.

Her hands were shaking badly as she reached out and took it from him, the action not losing its significance on her. By entrusting it to her, he was making himself vulnerable. Slowly taking the letter out of the envelope, she noted the London address.

Chrissie,

I need to see you and I deserve to see my son—you can't shut me out of his life like this. Your parents have no right to do this to us. I'm asking you to please give me another chance and let me see our wee bairn and you. I know I screwed up, but all I'm asking is for one more chance. I promise to make good this time. At least call me and let's meet somewhere so we can talk. Please.

Tommy.

He broke into the silence. "What do you think? Should I send it?"

"I would. It's important for families to be together, and you should get to see your son." Her voice held the slightest tremor. And yet she was strangely numb, like she was watching the scene play out from a distant point.

Tommy took out the packet of smokes and pulled one out, produced a lighter from another pocket in his jeans, and lit up. Taking a long drag on the cigarette, he offered it to her. She reached out with a shaking hand, took the cigarette, and brought it to her lips. Pain pierced them where her teeth had punctured her lip. She inhaled while contemplating her new weapon.

I could burn him, but I doubt I could get away with it and it's likely he'd turn nasty again. Best I wait.

He lit another one.

She looked at the cigarette in her hand and saw the red bloodline around the filter. She drew the smoke deep into her lungs and took comfort from the feeling.

"Your accent—what is it?" Tommy asked.

"I'm from New Zealand," she replied. *Keep talking.* "Do you know where New Zealand is?"

"I think it's somewhere near Australia." Seeing her nod, he took the bait. "What're you doing here?"

"I'm on my OE. Overseas experience. I'm here in Lesmahagow because it's where my grandmother was born." Wanting to make the point that she wasn't alone here, she continued. "I'm visiting my relations here. I've lots of aunts and uncles and cousins in the village."

"What's New Zealand like?" He appeared to be calming down. "I travelled about a lot with the Navy but I never got to go there."

"Well ..." Rose told him about New Zealand. It was a ridiculous scenario—here she was, having been assaulted by this stranger, giving a monologue about the wonders of the New Zealand landscape. But she needed to keep him talking.

Rose ground the cigarette butt under her foot. It was time to try and reason with him, so she made her plea. "Look, I'd better go. My uncle knows I'm on this path taking a photo and he'll be coming to look for me if I don't get back soon." She was at his mercy and he had power over her, the power of life or death.

Please let me go.

He looked at her with his head slightly to one side, obviously weighing up what she'd said.

It was crunch time.

"Well, if you promise no' to tell anyone about me or what happened here, I guess I can let you go."

Relief flooded through her. Yet she still felt detached, as if she was a third party watching their interplay, removed from it all. At the same time, she realised she was chilled to the bone, and shaking. She drew on all her remaining strength to retain control, to try and keep her composure. So close now to getting back to safety, she couldn't afford to blow it by giving him a reason to hurt her again. She welcomed the feeling of detachment.

"You can't go back looking like that," he said, pointing to her neck.

She looked down, and saw the blood was drying on her shirtfront.

He continued, "Ach, you've blood all over your face and neck." Taking out a large white hanky, he spat on it and gestured towards her head.

Like a little bird caught by the cat and subjected to its merciless play while unable to escape, she stood there in shocked stillness and allowed him to dab at the blood on her forehead, chin and neck. Terror prickled at the back of her neck and she prayed.

Lord, help me.

They stood there for what seemed like a long time. He was spitting on that hanky and dabbing at her neck, while she stood as still as death and allowed him to do so. Perhaps it was a power play to renew her terror, yet she just felt emptiness.

"Remember, if you tell anyone or go to the coppers, I promise I'll come and find you and finish you off. And be sure that I will find you." He eyeballed her for what seemed an eternity before turning and heading back along the path.

She held her breath and watched him until he was out of sight, until she was sure he wasn't coming back, until she was sure it was over and she was safe. Slowly she let her breath out. *Was it really over?* She picked her camera up from where it'd been flung. Then she fled back along the path, fearful he would come after her, running harder and faster as panic fuelled her, only vaguely aware of the attention she was attracting from passers-by. Tears of fear and relief made their way down her face and she could barely see where she was going.

Down Langdykeside, across into Bakers Brae and up the hill, desperate to reach the sanctuary of Ted's house.

4

Tommy left the New Zealand woman on the track and turned back to head for home. He walked quickly, eager to get away. He couldn't go to the Post Office now. With trembling hands, he put the blood-smeared envelope back in his pocket.

Chrissie, what have I done?

The familiar feeling of panic crept over him and he pulled his jacket closer around him, as if to find anonymity amongst its folds. The deep sense of dread sat in the pit of his stomach and rose up through his body, wave after wave, paralysing his thoughts and taking him captive without mercy. The racing of his pulse brought beads of sweat to his brow. The sound of his pounding chest echoed in his ears and he gasped to catch his breath as he became light-headed and dizzy. But then the haze began to clear and the pounding diminished.

Oh gawd, what was I thinking? What on earth came over me?

It was scary how he'd just snapped, losing control over his actions, becoming lost in the moment. Seeing the life slowly beginning to ebb away from her had almost felt good. At first it'd been fascinating, as if he had some sort of superpower, but now it disgusted him to know what he was capable of. Sure, he had been in plenty of fights in his time, but this was different—this was unprovoked. And never before had he attacked a stranger for no reason, let alone a defenceless woman.

How on earth had it happened? Why?

He couldn't recall coming across her on the track. The first thing he remembered was her trying to speak while looking over her shoulder and into his eyes. He could picture himself on her back, his hands around her throat and mouth, trying to squeeze the life out of her. And he'd nearly succeeded.

He tasted bile as a rush of nausea overtook him, and he threw up into the long grass. Spent, tears prickled his eyes and he coughed as the acid burned his throat. He dropped onto his haunches, hung his head in his hands and allowed the tears to flow. He pulled out his hanky to wipe his face, but it was all bloody.

A new wave of panic squeezed his gut. He stuffed the hanky back into his pocket and wiped his eyes and mouth with his sleeve.

Strewth, what have I done? I could've finished her off. Just a few more minutes and it would've been all over. Her eyes. I can see those blue eyes burning into me, pleading me to stop. Can I ever forget those eyes? Or will they forever haunt me?

He pulled out a lighter and the packet of fags. Put a fag to his mouth. Cupped his hands around it and lit up, finding calm in the familiar routine. He sucked the smoke in deep. It felt good, and he savoured it. After putting the packet and lighter back in his pocket he set off again, up the steep path towards the estate and his house. Yet his hands still shook as he dragged away on the fag.

Even after he'd hurt her, she'd been nice. She'd listened when he'd talked about his problems and she even seemed to care.

Aye, she was just an innocent stranger. And what am I—a murderer? She was here on holiday, for goodness sake—what sort of a holiday jaunt was that?

Well, at least he wouldn't have to see her around. Her injuries were probably superficial—cuts, grazes, swollen lips. The blood running down her throat ...

But what deviant monster attacks a complete stranger?

He looked down at his hands again and saw dried blood, concentrated around his bitten nails. *If only I hadn't decided to go to the Post Office.* Once again a wave of panic rose up from the pit of his stomach. A strange quickening sensation cast a shadow of fear over him. It wasn't real. Nothing was real. *What have I done?*

He had to think. Would she go to the cops? If she did, she'd describe him and it wouldn't be hard for them to work out who'd done it. Sure, he'd deny everything, but they wouldn't believe him. He'd had a few run-ins with the local coppers and it was a small village. His fiery temper was common knowledge, and no one believed it was never his fault. He couldn't go to prison, he just couldn't. It'd be worse than the Navy.

Staying low would be the best plan, just in case the cops came snooping. Or perhaps he'd go far away, somewhere where it'd be hard for them to find him. Morocco? Nay. No money and he could hardly ask Da' for a loan. London? Aye, that was it—he'd go back to London. He could catch the morning bus. In the meantime, he'd find Jimmy. Jimmy would help him stay out of the way of the coppers.

Tommy finished his fag and flicked the butt onto the path. Now he felt better. A drink would go down well about now. And Jimmy would be keen to go to the pub. He'd help drown out the whole stupid mess.

The track joined the street and he followed it along until he came to a house with a white Citroën GS parked outside, his dad's pride and joy. He grinned as he thought about how Da' had shown off the hydraulic suspension when he brought it home, sitting in front of the house, car going up and down as only a Citroën could.

He had moved back here after he and Chrissie had broken up. The two-storey terraced house was cramped, but it was free and you don't turn down free when you don't have work. Even if it meant living with Ma and Da' rowing all the time. Many times he'd slipped out the single vertical slide windows to escape his dad's foul mood.

Smoke curled from the chimney stack—someone was home. As if anyone could call this dingy pile of bricks home. He skipped over the wooden picket fence that separated the small front yard from the street, its chalky white paint beginning to flake. The fence had a paling missing—Da' had broken it across his legs one day for he couldn't remember what. Just another walloping. He was always being punished for doing stuff all.

He slunk across the small front yard where he used to kick a ball about and up the concrete path. It was amusing to think the house was a bit like his family—sound and tidy on the outside, but if you looked a little closer you could see the cracks. His dad was a lucky one who'd kept a good job, but even so there wasn't much to show for it.

He entered the house.

"Tommy, is that you?" Ma called out from sanctuary of the kitchen.

"Aye, be there soon." Tommy tore upstairs to the bathroom where he closed the door behind him, flicked the lock, crossed to the basin and looked in the mirror. The face that stared back at him looked gaunt and scared. It disgusted him.

He ran the hot water, filling the sink, then pulled the bloody hanky out of his pocket and dropped it in. The water, slowly turning crimson, was mesmerising. Then the reality of what he'd done hit. Again. Hairs prickled on the back of his neck as panic engulfed him.

He looked one last time at the dried blood on his shaking hands before plunging them into the hot water and scrubbing them with the nail brush. The sodden hanky seemed to stay a dirty colour no matter how much he rubbed and rinsed it. In disgust he flung it into the dirty laundry basket. He splashed cold water over his face, desperate to purge it of the memory. With one last look at his reflection to make sure he hadn't missed any blood, he went into his bedroom to change his clothes before going downstairs to the kitchen.

The room was warm and comforting, with a lingering smell of fresh baking. His mum sat at the table with a magazine open and a cup of tea in her hand. Being a petite woman, she'd always seemed so vulnerable—an easy victim.

"Awrite, Tommy?"

"Aye. What's there to eat?" he replied, scanning the bench.

"I've made a batch of oatcakes, over there under the towel." Ma pointed. "Cuppa?"

"Nay, I'm off out to catch Jimmy."

"What, again? Don't be late home this time and don't you go getting into any trouble. You know how your father is."

"I'm thinking of heading back to London in the morning."

"Really? Has Chrissie been in touch, then? How's the bairn?"

Hearing a note of concern in her voice, he studied her face and saw the look of sympathy as she observed him. Da' had always accused Tommy of being her laddie and he'd always loved the way she'd look at him, eyes twinkling. But when did she get to be so old? Her once-pretty face looked haggard, the deep worry lines hinting at a hard life. He resented Da' for that. She didn't deserve all the crap that he dished out.

Jolting himself back from his thoughts, he said, "I dunno, but I want to sort things out. I'll catch the bus in the morning."

"How long will you be gone this time?"

"Dunno. We'll just see how things go. I don't plan to come back up here for a while."

"Well if you're going out with Jimmy, you'd best get going before your Da' comes home. There's no after school meeting today, so I expect he'll be home soon."

"Aye, best I get going then." He went over and kissed her on the cheek before turning to go out the front door.

He skulked down the path, paranoid the cops might be waiting. Seeing nobody about, he turned onto the pavement and tried to hide inside his hooded sweatshirt, worried his face would reveal his guilt. Not too far down the street was Jimmy's house, the same as his but with a small tended flower garden out front. This house had always been his safe haven. Jimmy was his best mate. They'd had their fair share of scrapes, but Jimmy always knew how to sort things out. He hurried up the path and banged on the door, confident Jimmy would be home.

"Hold your horses!" Jimmy called swinging open the door and grinning from ear to ear. "Awrite, Tommy?"

"Aye. And you?"

"Ha, better for seeing you. What's up?"

"No' much." Tommy followed Jimmy inside, closing the door, relieved to be shutting out the world. He paused. Should he tell Jimmy the truth? Best not to. He couldn't risk it—even with Jimmy. It had to be his secret and his alone. It would be the first time he'd kept a secret from his friend and it dawned on him that this secret was a burden he'd have to carry for life. "I'm thinking it's high time we got plastered."

Jimmy laughed. "Aye, now that sounds like a plan. Did you hit the jackpot or something?"

"If only. Nay mate, it's all the crap happening just now. I'm thinking of heading back to London in the morning to see Chrissie."

"Aye, have you heard from her then?"

"Nay, but I need to move closer. I'll talk to Chrissie—maybe she'll see me again." Tommy scowled, still raw from her rejection.

"That girl's got some spunk if you ask me. Now, what about that bloody drink?" Jimmy winked at him. "Shall I see what the old man's got in stock?"

"What're we waiting for?"

Jimmy went out the back and returned with a jar of home brew. He poured the brown liquid into a couple of generous glasses and handed one to Tommy. They moved into the cluttered but cheerful sitting room. Tommy flopped onto one of the oversized armchairs, took out his packet of fags and went to offer one to Jimmy. But the memory of offering one to the girl on the path made him stop, made his hands shake. "What's wrong?" Jimmy eyed him with interest as he reached out and took the fag from him.

"Nothing." Tommy took one and lit it before passing the lighter to Jimmy. They supped and smoked in silence for a few minutes.

Tommy studied his near-spent fag. "It sucks, don't it?"

"What does?"

"Life. I mean, look at us. What's there to look forward to? We've no jobs, no money, no wife—and I've lost my bairn. What's the bloody point?"

"Ach, you're a long time dead." Jimmy landed a friendly punch on his shoulder. "Anyway, nobody's got any jobs round here."

"Aye, but I want more than that. Da's always banging on 'bout how useless I am and I hate that he's right." Tommy took a long drink and sighed.

"Now you listen here, Tommy Stewart. You ain't useless. Your da's the useless bloody one. He's been knocking you and your ma about for as long as I can remember. He's some poor excuse for a father, hiding behind his teaching and acting like he's all respectable and the like. The fact is, there's no jobs round here and we just got to accept it. Besides, we get by."

Tommy didn't respond. Deep in thought, he sipped his beer and contemplated his dad. One of his earliest memories was sitting at the table when Da' whacked him so hard on the back of the head that his head hit the table with a thump, splitting his lip. Ma told the doctor he'd crashed off his scooter. He can't have been very old, because the table had seemed huge back then. Another time, he was playing catch in the front yard with Da' and his older brother, Eric. Tommy kept dropping the ball until Da' lost his temper and dragged him inside and thumped him well and proper. Even now, the humiliation stung. Later when confined to his room, Ma had brought him his dinner on a tray, telling him it was their secret and not to tell Da'. His life had been a continuous charade of trying to please Da' and having to defend himself from him. How many times had he taken a beating? How often had he been told he was useless and a disappointment? How many times had he cowered in his bedroom listening to him hit Ma? "Da' made a success of his life—he's always had a job."

"Jobs don't make a man a success, no' if he treats his family bad."

Again they retreated into silence. A family portrait took pride of place on the wall in its big fancy frame. Why couldn't his family have been more like Jimmy's? There wasn't one thing that made him proud of who he was. He was nobody and he had nothing. He'd become a bully just like his dad. No, he was even worse than Da'—he was a bloody thug.

Jimmy interrupted his thoughts. "I hear Johnny Scott got a job driving trucks in Glasgow."

"Aye, he's a lucky one." Tommy took another sup. "Maybe I shouldn't have left the Navy. At least I had a job, and the pay wasn't bad. Three free cans of beer a day weren't too bad either."

"Aren't you forgetting something? You hated the Navy."

"It was good getting about. We saw a lot of places— never got to see New Zealand though."

"Now that's a strange thing to say. What's New Zealand got to do with anything?" Jimmy eyed Tommy curiously.

Tommy paused. Should he tell? "Nothing. I just hear it's a real nice place to visit."

Tommy drained his glass and Jimmy followed suit, then refilled them. Again they lapsed into silence, broken only by the occasional slurp and the sound of a glass bumping onto the small centre table. Tommy studied his trembling hands, sickened by the sight of them. What had he done? What if he hadn't stopped? He could almost feel that moment... He shuddered and took another sip.

"Have you ever thought about killing someone?" Tommy asked. "Do you think you could? Have you ever thought about what it would be like?"

"What are you talking about Tommy Stewart? You're nuts!"

"Aye, maybe I am. Who'd know?" Tommy sighed. "I'm bad news Jimmy, worse than Da'. I don't know what I'm capable of, but I know it's no good."

"You're talking nonsense."

"I'm no good Jimmy—and I don't deserve Chrissie."

"That's rubbish. What's brought all this on then?"

"Don't worry. Forget it." Tommy drained his glass.

Jimmy picked up the empty jar. "Another? Sounds to me like you need it." He went out and came back in with a full one and refilled the glasses. "So what's your plan for Chrissie? How will you deal with her parents?"

"I dunno—it's hopeless. Her parents think I'm no' good enough and I guess they're right."

"Nay, don't think that. You'll need to get a job down there to prove them wrong."

"What's the chance of that? What can I do? I've no skills. My time in the Navy was a fat lot of use—what can an able seaman do round here?" He scowled at his glass.

"Don't be so hard on yourself."

"Yeah? So where's my job?" Tommy sighed. "I want to see my bairn—he's the best thing I've ever done. You know, he's six months old now?"

"Aye, so he is."

"I miss Chrissie's singing. I miss her smile. How can I live without them? It doesn't even seem like it's worth getting up in the mornings. I need them, Jimmy."

"Aye, don't you worry. I reckon—" The sound of persistent knocking on the front door interrupted him.

Panic consumed Tommy. "Don't answer it."

"Don't be daft."

Tommy jumped up. "Tell them you haven't seen me."

"Tell who? What's going on?"

Knock, knock, knock.

"I've done something. I've got to hide."

"Go up to my room and I'll deal with whoever it is."

What have I done?

He darted up the stairs, then stood quietly in the doorway to Jimmy's room trying to hear the events below over the noise of his own beating heart. Waiting, he couldn't help but hold his breath as Jimmy opened the door downstairs.

"Hello, Mr Stewart," Jimmy announced loudly for Tommy's benefit.

Not the constable, then. Only his da'. Elation flooded through Tommy as he breathed a welcome sigh of relief. His muscles relaxed as he grinned at the irony of feeling relief at the sound of his dad's voice.

"Hello Jimmy. Is Tommy here? I need to talk to him."

"Come on in, Mr Stewart." The front door shut and there were footsteps into the sitting room. "Tommy, it's your da!"

Making his way down the stairs, Tommy wondered what his dad might want. It was unusual for him to come round to Jimmy's. But at least his secret was safe. For now.

His dad gave a mean look, obviously in one of his foul moods. "I hear you're heading back down to London."

"Aye."

"And just what do you think you'll be doing in London?"

"I'll find some work."

"And just who do you think would want to employ you?"

"Ach, leave me alone. I'll sort it."

"You'll sort it? Like you sorted the mess you made of Chrissie and your son? You've never managed to do one thing right in your whole useless life. If only you were more like your brother. But no, you've too much of your mother in you. You're a useless good-for-nothing poor-excuse-for-a-son if ever I saw one."

Crushed by the familiar ranting, but not wanting to show it, Tommy stood tall and tried to look staunch.

"Well, what have you got to say for yourself?" Da' stood, legs astride with hands on hips.

"I—nothing." Tommy couldn't look him in the eye.

"Good gracious! How does an English teacher end up with such an idiot for a son? How many times have I tried to teach you to speak properly? What must people think of us, if I can't even teach my own son?"

Bristling, Tommy thought of the beatings he'd endured as a lad, all because he'd messed up his sentences. *Bastard!*

"I've given you everything you ever needed—a roof over your head and food in your belly. But since you've been back, never once have you shown any gratitude or gotten off your backside to go out and find real work to pay your way. And now you're going to just bugger off again and no doubt make more mess and bring more shame to our family name."

"Whoa, Mr Stewart, that's a bit unfair."

Da' turned to glare at Jimmy. "Jimmy Brown, I'll thank you no' to get involved in our family business." Turning his attention back to Tommy, he added, "Look at you, you've been drinking again. Don't bother to come back home until you sort your life out for once and for all. I'm tired of your charades. Why don't you take a leaf out of your brother's book?" With that he turned and walked through the hall and out the front door, slamming it in his wake.

A hand squeezed his shoulder and Tommy turned to face Jimmy, and scowled. "I hate my Da'. I wish he were dead." Retreating to the couch, he picked up his glass—hoping to find some comfort.

"Aye, best you head for London. Your old man's a nutter." Jimmy picked up a packet of fags and offered one to Tommy. "What was all that hiding about?"

Tired and now vulnerable, Tommy sat for a long moment with his head in his hands. He had no fight left. "Don't ask—you really don't want to know."

There was a long pause.

Tommy looked up and saw the hurt expression on his friend's face and he knew he owed him more of an explanation. "I done something dumb today. Don't know what came over me, but I hurt someone, a girl. The cops will probably come looking for me. I've got to get out o' Lesmahagow."

"What do you mean, hurt her?"

"Don't ask. If they come round, the less you know the better. Jimmy, you're my best mate and we've always been there for each other. Just help me stay out of their way. And help me sort things with Chrissie. I've got to get to London as soon as I can."

"Holy crap, Tommy. You're an idiot." Jimmy looked pensive. "Maybe we should lie low here for a bit before picking up your things. Your da's in a right mood. Aye, I'll see that you get on that bus. And you know you can trust me to keep my mouth shut with the coppers."

5

Rose rounded the corner, puffed and sweaty, to see Ted kneeling in front of the flower garden outside his house. As she approached he turned to face her, his broad smile was immediately replaced by a deep frown. "My gawd child, what's happened to you?"

"I've been attacked." She unravelled, like a great knitted garment. Her sobs became uncontrollable, replacing her earlier bravery. The fear was raw and all consuming, knotting up her stomach as if being squeezed by a great fist.

"Come inside, lass. We'll need to call the police." He shepherded her indoors and through to the sitting room where he motioned towards the couch before leaving the room.

Returning, he said, "The police are on their way. And I've asked Agnes to come over and tend to you."

She hung her head, too distraught to answer.

Ted hovered about her as if he was uncomfortable having a distressed damsel to deal with. "What can I do, lass?"

"Nothing, I'm okay, thanks."

"Should I put a call through to your mother?"

"No, please don't do that. I don't want to worry them."

Agnes, another of her mother's cousins, arrived in a flurry. "Ach Rose, poor child. What a mess. When Ted called, I couldn't believe it. Are you in any pain?"

"I'll be okay, thanks." Rose managed a limp smile, even as her lip quivered and she fought back fresh tears.

"Let me make you a hot drink to help calm your nerves." Agnes glanced at Ted. "Can you get me a bottle of your best whisky?" She followed him out of the room.

Rose closed her eyes, wishing she'd never gone for that walk. Had never taken that photo. If only the whole thing would just go away. *If only I was home.*

Agnes came back a few minutes later with a steaming mug and a towel slung over her forearm. Ted trailed behind carrying two more mugs and passed one to Rose. "This will help."

"Thanks."

Grateful for the diversion, Rose took the mug and cautiously raised it to her lips. She winced and put it back down to let it cool a little. Agnes passed her the towel and Rose tried to dab her wounds to stop the blood, which was still oozing in places.

After she'd given the drink a chance to cool a little, she took another sip, drawing comfort from the hot toddy. She savoured its sweetness and could feel the generous dram of Ted's whisky seep through her veins as it warmed her from the inside.

Agnes reminded Rose of her mother and her tension eased. Agnes had a gentle and calm spirit, which was just what Rose needed right now, and she was relieved to surrender herself into Agnes's care.

A car sounded on the drive, and the man's words came back to Rose.

Remember, if you tell anyone or go to the coppers, I promise I'll come and find you and finish you off. And be sure that I will find you.

Ted ushered in a uniformed policeman. She guessed he was around fifty, with an intimidating tall and burly appearance that typified men in his occupation.

"Rose, meet Sergeant Moffat. This is Rose." Ted gestured towards a chair. "Take a seat."

"Rose." Sergeant Moffat pulled up a dining chair to sit opposite her and took out his notepad and pen.

Rose didn't speak.

"What's your full name, address and date of birth?"

As Rose answered, he made notes. She gave her London address.

"So what appears to be the problem here?" His dark eyes bored into her. His expression sombre.

She wilted under their gaze as they waited expectantly for her to respond. Once more the dark clouds threatened to engulf her and she took a deep breath. "I was taking a picture of the village along the old railway track when someone jumped me from behind and tried to strangle me." The tremor in her voice betrayed her struggle to control her emotions, and Agnes placed her arm lightly around her shoulders.

"Hmmm." His pen moved quickly on the notepad. "What did your alleged attacker look like?"

Really? Alleged? Does he think I did this to myself?

"I don't know." *If I tell he could come back to finish me off.* Thinking fast, she went on, "He came from behind and

I didn't see him. I think I must've blacked out, because I can't remember a whole lot—and then he was gone."

It was a lie and Rose hated lying. But she had no choice. She looked down at her hands fidgeting in her lap. *If I tell the truth, could the man find out and come after me? Maybe tonight when it was dark? If the police visit him today—will they arrest him? Probably not. Best to stay safe and say nothing.* She turned to Agnes, desperate for the older woman's wisdom. But she was alone in this. *What if the police find out I've lied?* A sudden wave of panic washed over her, threatening to overwhelm her. She gulped as if trying to submerge it. *Maybe it's better to lie to the police than have that man find me.*

"Did he sexually assault you?" He twisted the end of the thick dark moustache that hid part of his upper lip.

Her cheeks flushed at the insensitive question. Crossing her arms she answered, "No, no not at all. H-he just seemed to want to strangle me."

"And are you sure you haven't met him before? Perhaps you met him at the pub over a drink?" He raised one eyebrow.

She resented the insinuation. "No, and I haven't been to the pub."

"What sort of build was he?"

"Maybe around the same as me." She was vague on purpose, her words weighed down by guilt. Lying didn't feel good.

"What was he wearing?"

"I-I don't know. I couldn't see him."

"Well, did he have jeans on?"

"I don't know." She twisted her hands in her lap.

"What footwear did he have?"

"I don't know."

"How did you get away?"

"I tried to fight and scream, but then I blacked out." The flaws in her story seemed too obvious. But the words had come fast and were purely instinctive and in the interests of self-preservation.

"Can you not remember anything that would help us find him?" This time there was a hint of exasperation in his voice.

"No." Again, the tears welled up and followed their now familiar route down her cheeks.

He pulled out what appeared to be a form and began to write, checking his notepad as he went. It was a welcome break from the questions.

"Rose, please check the statement is correct and sign it here." He passed it to her and indicated the space at the bottom.

She read it and hesitated, unsure what her rights were. Unsure of the consequences. Unsure she was doing the right thing. Then she scribbled her signature.

"You're not from around these parts. Where're you from?"

"New Zealand. I'm here visiting family."

"Hmmm, well then, I'll need to sketch your injuries and then I'll be off and leave you to rest." He studied Rose with renewed interest and the pen scratched away busily on the page. A few minutes later he was closing his pad and preparing to leave. "Your neck and lips are a mess, lass. Best get cleaned up before infection sets in."

Agnes took over. "I was going to dress the wounds but thought we had best wait until you arrived."

"Yes, I remember you were a nurse," he said. "Keep a close eye on her now—she's had quite an ordeal and you'll need to watch out for delayed shock."

"Of course we will."

Sergeant Moffat turned back to Rose. "You haven't given us much to go on, but I'll see what we can do. Call the station if you remember anything else." He gathered his things, stood up and nodded to Ted. They both left the room.

"Come through with me to the bathroom and I'll clean and dress those wounds," Agnes said.

Rose allowed Agnes to gently guide her through the hallway and into the bathroom, an arm around her shoulders.

"Wait here a wee bit and I'll get a towel and the first aid box." Agnes disappeared out the door.

Numb and vacant, Rose stared at her reflection in the mirror until Agnes returned with towels and a box of dressings.

"Poor child." Agnes muttered.

She filled the sink with hot water and a healthy amount of antiseptic and set to work dabbing the back of Rose's head where the bloodied and matted hair exposed the lump and gash where the rock had hit. Although Agnes' touch was gentle, Rose winced at the sharp combination of hot water and antiseptic.

"Ach, who would do such a thing?" Agnes moved to the lump and gash on her forehead. "He needs to be locked away."

When Agnes had finished, Rose took the cloth and dabbed at her swollen, cut lips, trying not to flinch at each touch. But her neck was the worst part. She could feel it swelling, where his thumb had gone through layers of skin and given her a deep flesh wound which continued to ooze. On the other side was a graze where his fingers had gripped into her skin. Below this was a trail of dried blood that went down to her shirt, leaving ugly smudges on the chequered cotton.

"Curse him!" Agnes pulled some dressings out of the box and applied them to the wounds on Rose's forehead and neck.

Rose looked down at her hands. They were still shaking, and the swelling in her throat was making swallowing difficult. Tears began to flow again.

"I'm so sorry, Agnes. I just can't seem to stop crying."

"Ach, there's no need to apologise. You'll be suffering from shock just now and it's only natural to be feeling this way. You've had a terrible ordeal, and it'll take some time to get over it."

Rose wiped her tears, feeling a wealth of gratitude for this angel who brought a ray of light into the darkness of her trauma and despair.

"There, I think we're done," Agnes said. "How about you go and put some clean clothes on? Maybe even have a lie down for a bit. You'll feel better for it."

*

Rose tried to nap but couldn't relax. She lay there staring at the ceiling until she couldn't bear it any longer. She could hear voices and she got up to find the sitting room full of people—some she'd met on her first night and others were strangers. Her attack was the hot topic. Throughout the afternoon they came and went and bombarded her with questions.

"Who did it?"

"What did he look like?"

"Where was the attack?"

"How did you get away?"

"Did you hurt him?"

It was exhausting. If only she could escape to her room but she couldn't be rude. She stuck to the story she'd told the policeman.

"I didn't see anything."

"I don't know who did it."

She hated the lies. Her heart beat rapidly in her chest and she sat, afraid she'd faint. *Will he come and get me?* Lying to the police had complicated things, but what could she do? She was caught in a trap that tightened with her every move.

A dozen or so men paced the small room, whipped into a frenzy of righteous anger.

"We need to see that justice is done," one of the older men said.

"I'll bet I know who did it," Andy said, his expression angry. "It'll be that good-for-nothing Tommy Stewart from the housing estate over the other side. He's trouble, that one. I say we go and teach him a lesson."

The other men in the room murmured in agreement and sounded intent on a bit of vigilante justice.

She listened in horror and her stomach tightened as a wave of nausea hit her. It was all her fault and now these newfound relatives were in danger of getting themselves into trouble. It wasn't right that she just sat back and let that happen. She would be responsible for their actions and she couldn't let them break the law on her behalf.

"No, please." She had to stop them. She had no idea how far they would go to protect 'one of their clan'.

The chatter stopped as they all looked at her.

"I don't know who it was—I didn't see anything. Please, just let it be. I don't want you to get into trouble on my account," she said.

The men continued to debate the possibility of going after her attacker themselves, but common sense took over.

"Andy, why don't you take Rose out for a wee drive and some dinner? Help the lass to take her mind off it," Ted said. "Ach it might cheer her up a bit."

As if it would. Still, it was better than sitting around listening to the men scheming and so Rose agreed to go with Andy.

A short time later Rose gingerly got into Andy's blue Mini. Her scrapes were hurting and her head was throbbing. She was relieved when Andy insisted that they head away from Lesmahagow and up to the Firth of Clyde to see the Forth Bridge. It was obvious he was trying hard to be the comic and cheer her up, but she wasn't in the mood.

She took the obligatory tourist photos to try and show her gratitude. Andy treated her to a takeaway meal of black pudding, haggis and tatties, but she could only pick at the food. Although she tried to wear a brave face, she was gripped by a shroud of fear and she was aware she wasn't good company. All she wanted was to be alone. When they finally arrived back at Ted's, she used the excuse of needing rest, and saw Andy off early.

She had planned to visit another cousin in the seaside town of Largs the next day and she was determined to go ahead, to escape Lesmahagow and Tommy.

After bidding Ted goodnight, Rose prepared for bed. Being a creature of habit, she took out her diary. She didn't want to relive the ordeal by putting it into words. If only she could forget about it—move on. She wrote:

After breakfast I went for a walk around the village and up the hill onto the path along the old railway tracks to get a good view of the village for a photo. It was there I was attacked. I went back to Ted's and had a cuppa with him and Agnes. The police came and went. Andy took me to see the Forth Bridge and we had takeaways of haggis, black pudding and tatties.

The house was silent, with only the occasional sound of cars in the distance. Rose sat up in bed with the light on and wept silently. Although knowing it to be ridiculous, she kept an eye on the curtains. Fearful. Expecting to see them part at any time and for him to emerge.

If only Gary was with her, to hold her and comfort her. But no. She was on her own. It wouldn't be any good going to Ted. He wouldn't know what to do and it would be awkward. And besides, she'd already caused him enough trouble.

Fear spread like a thick dark cloud, filling her spirit with a profound sense of dread. Exhausted as she was, she dared not allow herself the luxury of sleep for fear Tommy would find her. Depressed and hurting all over, she sat motionless and upright, her back to the wall, with the light on.

And the hours dragged on.

Eventually, she became restless. She got out of bed and went over to the mirror above the dressing table. The image that stared back was freakish and barely recognisable. Her throat was now badly swollen, and her neckline was hidden by bulging flesh that protruded over her jawbone. Her face looked hideous, and the swelling completely obscured the outline of her jaw. Her lips were bloated, cut and sore where she'd bitten through them. Her eyes were panda eyes; glassy and bloodshot eyeballs nestled in dark rings. She lifted her top to reveal more bruising. The reality of what she saw hit her once more, and the tears flowed, dripping off her face and onto the dresser.

She tiptoed back to bed so as not to wake Ted in the next room. With the window shut, she continued her tearful vigil. And the night slowly passed.

*

Breakfast was awkward, with Ted seeming to be at a loss over how to relate to her. Miserable and increasingly irritable, she tried not to show it. Her head throbbed and she ached all over. And she could do with some sleep.

After packing up her things, Ted drove her to Glasgow to catch the ten fifteen train to Largs. They drove along in silence and she was thankful for the quiet. As the miles distanced her from Lesmahagow, her relief at escaping the scene of her trauma increased. Right now, she hoped never to return.

They pulled into the station car park.

"Thanks so much for all you've done over the last few days. It was great getting to know you." Rose knew she had to be polite, no matter how much she wanted to make her escape.

"Ach Rose, I'm just sorry for what you went through. Our wee village is normally such a quiet place—I just don't understand it."

"Look, don't worry. I was just in the wrong place at the wrong time. But I'm okay. Really. I'd better go. Bye, and thanks again."

"Aye, lass. Bye for now. Let me know how you get on."

As she climbed out of the car, she scanned the car park, half expecting to see Tommy. In a daze, she bought her ticket at the ticket office and located the right platform. The train was already there, so she hurried towards the last carriage, hoping it would have fewer passengers.

She surveyed the carriage before taking a forward-facing seat halfway down the carriage, which gave her a vantage point over both doors. As they waited to depart, she kept a wary eye on the exits—in case Tommy boarded.

Finally, the doors closed. Her head jerked back as the train pulled out of the station, and she winced at the sudden painful movement. Every few minutes she twisted her throbbing head around, scared Tommy would come at her from behind. Once more she found herself weeping, vaguely aware of the stares of the strangers around her, but not really caring.

Thinking through the events of the past day, she pondered the consequences of having lied in her statement to the police. Did this make her guilty of perjury? She hadn't sworn any oath. Nevertheless, she'd better put it right before she ended up in trouble with the law. Perhaps she could report it in Largs, where the threat of Tommy finding her was more remote.

An hour of worrying passed before the train pulled into Largs. Relieved, she spied Meg, her mother's cousin, waiting on the platform. Meg's was a familiar face—Rose had met her and her husband, John, in New Zealand and had liked them immensely. Meg was a bright and attractive woman in her mid-fifties. A slim blonde, she held herself straight and tall and was dressed in smart tartan trousers and a light sweater. When Meg spotted Rose, she waved, her face beamed a welcoming smile. Rose hurried out to greet her.

"It's so lovely to meet you again, Rose." Meg's voice had a beautiful lyrical inflection that attested to years of elocution training. She paused and studied Rose. "You look terrible. Ted called and told me what happened, but I didn't expect it to be so bad."

"Meg, I've done something really terrible." Tears welled up and spilled onto her cheeks. "I've committed perjury. I need to go to the police station."

"There, Rose. Let me take you home and make you a hot drink, and you can tell me all about it." Meg's tone was calm yet authoritative, and before Rose could protest, Meg had picked up her bag and was leading her off the platform towards the car park.

*

Meg's bungalow was bright and welcoming. Rose followed her into a sitting room decorated with Laura Ashley-style floral wallpaper and one wall had a floor-to-ceiling bookcase stuffed full of books. She was drawn to a large window overlooking the sea and islands.

"What's the name of that island?" She pointed to the nearest.

"Great Cumbrae. And that one in the distance is Arran. If you look carefully you might be able to make out the outline of a man lying on his back with his arms folded over his chest."

"Oh yes, I can see it," Rose said. "I love the sea. I think it has such a calming effect."

"Aye, we love it too. In fact, John loves to sail—perhaps he can take you out after work? It would do you good."

"I'd love to." She took a seat on the pale green sofa plumped up with cushions.

Meg made Rose a hot tea and slipped in a dram of finest Scotch whisky. Rose gratefully accepted it, along with the tissues Meg offered. Rose sipped her tea slowly, avoiding the sorest parts of her lips while allowing the hot liquid to warm her inside.

Meg sat opposite with pen and paper in hand, as if she were a detective. "Right. How about you start from the beginning and I'll take notes. Then, when we're done, I'll take you down to the police station."

Rose reached for a tissue and blew noisily, then related her story, taking care not to leave anything out. Tears flowed, but she ignored them and continued with her monologue, determined to get to the end.

"So you see." Rose looked at Meg, who seemed to be enjoying her self-appointed role. "I'm scared that I'm now guilty of perjury, and I don't want to get in any trouble with the police."

"I understand, but you haven't committed an offense. You've been in shock and have just reacted in a way that was natural for you to protect yourself," Meg said. "I'll call the police station here and see if we can go down there and meet with one of the officers." She went over to the phone to make the call.

With Meg's support the load had lifted, and Rose sank back into the comfortable sofa, closing her eyes. Exhausted, she had to force herself to stay awake.

*

Within the hour, they were sitting in the office of Sergeant Bob Campbell. Sergeant Campbell was tall and of a solid build with a fatherly demeanour that put Rose at ease. His face creased in ready smiles and his eyes twinkled with friendly encouragement that belied his position.

Once again, Rose poured out her story, but this time with Meg occasionally interrupting to fill in a detail from her notepad. Rose pushed on, ignoring her tears. Sergeant Campbell made copious notes, stopping every now and then to ask a question to help draw the story out. Finally, she was finished.

"I'm really sorry I didn't tell the whole truth in Lesmahagow. I never intended to lie in my statement, but I was scared. I hope it hasn't caused any problems."

"Rose, don't you worry about that," the sergeant said. "This is a fairly normal reaction, and I see it over and over again. It's not unusual for a female victim of violence to try to protect her attacker out of fear of retribution. You've been going through post-trauma shock and it's a natural reaction. Shock can be a strange bedfellow—it manifests itself in different ways with different people."

"I'm afraid it's all new to me," Rose said as a fresh wave of tears started to roll their way down her cheeks.

"Well, I'm so sorry you've had to go through this here in Scotland," he said as he toyed with his pen. "I'll pass this on to the Lesmahagow police. Are you willing to press charges?"

"I... I don't know." She contemplated the options. "I don't think I hate him, although I hate what he did to me, but I kind of feel sorry for him. I don't really want to see him go to prison, but I do want him to get some sort of psychiatric help so that this doesn't happen to anyone else." It occurred to her that until that moment, she had been so focused on her own feelings that she hadn't been aware of the depth of her pity for Tommy.

Sergeant Campbell dropped his pen on the table and looked at her for a long moment, his brow furrowed in concentration.

"Rose, I want to talk to you off the record, like," Sergeant Campbell said, his voice quieter now. "Please understand I'm not supposed to say this, but I want to give you some advice, so please don't quote me. If you were my daughter, I would say to you..." He paused, as if unsure whether to continue.

He had her full attention.

"I would tell you not to press charges," he said. "You're here on your gap year and this would ruin that experience.

Instead, complete your year of travel and have some positive experiences so you take good memories home. Go to Europe as you've planned, have the backpacking holiday, and try to forget this episode. Put it down to being in the wrong place at the wrong time."

"What would happen if I press charges?"

"Ah, assuming this man—" He paused to check his notes. "Assuming Tommy is apprehended by the Lesmahagow police, and assuming he pleads not guilty, then the prosecutor will probably decide there's a case to answer. Because of the serious nature of this assault, it's likely it will go to the Crown Court and not the Magistrates Court. As the main witness, you'll need to stay in the UK until the trial is over—perhaps six months or even a year."

"I can't afford to stay that long," Rose said. "My return ticket is in six months and I want to go home."

"It's how long it takes. At the trial, you'll be cross-examined in the witness box. Your character will come under scrutiny, even though you're the victim. I hate to say it, and again strictly off the record, you'll also be the foreigner in the trial. All in all, it'll not be a positive experience and frankly, I would advise my daughter not to press charges. Let the local police have a talk to him and then keep close tabs on him. They can get him help."

Rose looked at Meg, who nodded her agreement. Rose looked back to the friendly sergeant. She knew his advice was wise and he spoke with her best interests at heart.

"That's exactly what I want, Sergeant Campbell. I want him to get help and I want to be sure he won't repeat the offense. I trust the local police will see to that once they know about him."

"Rose, I'm sure you're making the right decision. You know, you're lucky to have survived this. By what you've told me, and looking at your injuries, you could easily have lost consciousness and then it's anyone's guess as to how this could have ended. We could be dealing with a whole different outcome, murder rather than assault. Trust me, you are one very lucky young lady—and one who can keep a cool head."

Fresh tears welled up and Rose dabbed her eyes with a tissue before blowing her nose.

Sergeant Campbell continued in more gentle tones, "I'm sorry, I didn't mean to upset you. But you are a brave young lady. I hope you will go and have a great time and take some happy memories home."

"Thanks. I'd planned to leave my job in London next month to start the trip around Europe before flying home to New Zealand in November. I really want this to be a memorable trip for all the right reasons. I don't want it ruined by this."

He scribbled some more and passed her a form to sign. She signed it.

"I'll get this statement through to the Lesmahagow police." Sergeant Campbell stood indicating the interview was over, and Rose and Meg followed suit. He put out his hand and Rose shook it. "Good luck Rose. And try to put this behind you."

"Thanks so much, Sergeant Campbell. I really do appreciate all the advice." She turned and left the office with Meg at her side.

*

After the police interview, Rose and Meg spent the afternoon at home. Meg insisted Rose take an afternoon nap and she soon succumbed to sleep. When she woke up, she found Meg in the kitchen preparing an early dinner.

"Rose, did you sleep?" Meg asked, as Rose entered the kitchen.

"Yes, thanks. I feel much better for it."

"That's good. We thought we'd have an early tea and John will take us out sailing. Would you like that?"

"Wow, that'd be great. I have to warn you, I'm a complete novice. You'll have to tell me what to do."

"Good, that's settled then. Don't worry—John will teach you the ropes. He's planning on coming home early, so he should be here any time now."

"Can I help?"

"Aye, you could make a wee salad." Meg took out some salad vegetables from the fridge and passed her a bowl, chopping board and knife.

Rose sliced some tomato. "Meg, I've been thinking about the rellies in Lesmahagow and I'm feeling bad about not telling them everything. I was just so afraid he'd come after me if I told the police—and then I didn't want them to go after my attacker and get themselves in trouble. But I hate lying."

"Don't worry, Rose. You were in shock."

"But I don't want to hurt them by lying to them. Would you mind if we just keep the bit about his identity to ourselves?"

"Well if you're sure. But they're good folks and would understand."

"I'd just prefer not to say anything. Would you mind?"

"Well, if that's what you want, we'll just let it be."

Rose was just putting the finishing touches on the salad when a car pulled up in the driveway and John entered the kitchen.

"Hello, Rose. Good to see you again. Has it really been three years since we were in New Zealand?" John smiled and gave her a hug before moving on to peck Meg on the cheek. He was a tall, slim man with a gentle nature and it was easy to feel safe and comfortable with him.

"It's good to see you and to be here at last. I've been looking forward to getting up to Scotland. It's been hard getting away from London as I only get one and a half days off a week." Rose was genuinely pleased to see him.

"I hear you've been in the wars. A sail will make you feel better—nothing like a bit of salt in the air," John said.

"I can't wait."

"Well, we'll get going as soon as we've had something to eat."

After their meal, John drove them down to the shore where they clambered aboard the small dinghy and headed out to where the yacht *Gypsy Lady* was moored. Rose loved the beautiful sleek lines of the craft that hinted at its ability to slip through the water. It was no wonder sailors referred to their ships as if they were feminine.

"She's beautiful," Rose said, turning to John.

"Aye, she is. She's what we call a sloop, a single mast yacht with two sails."

"How far have you been on her?"

"We sail the Firth of Clyde as often as we can get away," Meg said. "Last summer, we sailed her to the Mediterranean and as far as Yugoslavia."

"Wow. Don't you get frightened when you get into big seas?"

"Nay, she's built to handle them and she does so with ease. You just need to be sensible about how much sail you have out. If it's a real gale, we just take shelter in a bay somewhere." John steered the dinghy towards the stern.

"I'd love to holiday cruising the Med."

"Well, perhaps one day you can. We love it—cruising is like being a gypsy on the sea. We don't like to plan too much—where we end up depends a lot on the weather."

"Is that why she's called *Gypsy Lady*?"

"Aye," John said. They pulled up alongside the sloop. "Hop on and welcome aboard."

They boarded and John tied the dinghy to the stern. After a tour of the cabin below deck, Meg untied the mooring buoy and they were underway. John called out instructions to Rose, who hauled on the ropes he called halyards and sheets. She moved with the pained and purposeful movements of an old woman, favouring her injuries as the unfamiliar and yet gentle rocking motion of the sea beneath her feet exacerbated her awkwardness. With sails set, they were soon under way.

The water quietly lapped the sides of the yacht and the wind caressed the sails. Rose found it easy to relax, her surroundings lulling her into a feeling of security and contentment. She breathed in the sea air, willing it to wash away the memories and fear. It was like the boat was a small island in a vast sea and she was safe—Tommy couldn't reach her here.

A seagull swooped down and she watched it soar and glide on the breeze, a magnificent sight. *Oh to be free like a bird, to be fearless and to run with the wind.*

As they meandered about, she became increasingly buoyed, inspired by the beautiful world around her. There was so much to live for.

6

London

Tommy looked at the imposing stained wooden door with the white trim, apprehensive, willing it to open and for Chrissie to be there. He took a deep breath and pulled himself up to his full height before reaching for the brass knocker.

Knock, knock, knock.

There were voices inside, but the sound was muffled.

Knock, knock, knock.

A chain rattled and the door opened up a crack. The face that appeared behind the door dashed his hopes.

"You're not welcome here Tommy Stewart," hissed Chrissie's mum.

"I'm here to see Chrissie—is she here?" Tommy tried to keep his voice steady.

"She doesn't want to see you. Now get out and don't come back around here again, do you hear me?"

"Please, Mrs Thomson, I just wanna talk. It won't take long." Desperation turned into anger as a baby cried inside. "Please let me see her! Now!"

"Stay away from her—she doesn't want to see you." She started to shut the door, then stopped and peered through it again as if a new thought had struck her. "I'm warning you, if I see you around here again, I'll call the police." She slammed the door.

Choosing to ignore her threat, he knocked again, hoping Chrissie would come to the door this time.

Knock, knock, knock.

"Go away." Muffled but audible, the message was clear.

"Sod you!" He shoved his hands in his pockets and turned to walk back up the driveway, kicking out at the small manicured border of hedging plants.

Now what? He had to think. Coming to the bus stop, he spied a rubbish bin and kicked it violently, cursing under his breath. His only chance of seeing Chrissie was if he could catch her when she left home. The house was in full view of the bus shelter and he decided to wait there. He had to see Chrissie, and he'd wait for hours if need be. And if she didn't come out today, he'd come back tomorrow and if not tomorrow, then the day after, and every day until he saw her. She'd have to come out some time.

Taking out his fags and lighter, he put one between his lips and lit up, drawing deeply on it. *Aye, it could be a long wait.* There weren't many people on the street and he guessed most were probably at work. Finchley was on London's Northern Line and this part of the city was definitely home to the more middle-class white-collar type. It was a prime location, near Brent Cross and not far from Barnet to the north and Hampstead to the south.

On one side of the street was a neat row of attached houses and on the other a mixture of semi-detached and fully-detached. They all looked so posh, located back from the street and with driveways intersecting clipped lawns. The gardens were obviously well-tended with leafy shrubs and trees, hinting at the general affluence of the inhabitants and their neighbourhood pride.

The Thomson's home was a two-storey terraced house, reddish brick with white trims. Struck by the contrast between this and his own family home, he felt a twinge of bitterness. *They think they're so much better than us.*

A woman came out of one of the houses with a small child in tow, and they moved towards him. Where was Chrissie? She should know he'd be out here. A bus rolled along towards him and came to a stop at the bus shelter. Its doors opened and the woman with the child boarded. The bus driver looked expectantly at him, then closed the doors and moved away, leaving him standing at the shelter.

Time dragged by. Still Tommy stood there, watching and waiting. Buses and people came and went. Clouds moved across the sun and then scurried away across the sky.

It had been good with Chrissie. They'd met while he was in the Navy. He'd been on shore leave and had come up to London for the weekend with his mate, Dobbo. They'd been sitting in a pub when he'd noticed her, a bonnie blue-eyed blonde with a glowing face and a dimple in her cheek when she smiled. How he loved that dimple.

They'd gone on to a nightclub and danced the night away. He'd loved the way her laughter bubbled at the least funny thing. She'd given him her number scribbled on a scrap of paper. Amazing. He'd never dreamed a classy lass like her could be interested in someone like him.

Hungry, he looked at his watch and saw it was mid-afternoon—he'd missed lunch. He pulled out his pack of fags and saw he was down to his last. *Strewth!* Irritated, he kicked some rubbish into the gutter. Should he give up?

Lighting up, he savoured the smoke like a dying man with his last meal.

A movement at the house caught his eye. The door was opening and Chrissie emerged, pushing a pram. He watched as she manoeuvred the pram down the steps and onto the path. He watched as she swayed her hips in that familiar and sensuous way. He watched as her thick curly blonde ponytail swung behind her as she walked. She was wearing a tee shirt and tight jeans, revealing her tall slim body had fully recovered from the pregnancy. The pram, his son. He was about to see his son.

As she turned into the street towards him, he was struck by a more sinister memory. Something about Chrissie reminded him of that New Zealand woman on the track in Lesmahagow—perhaps it was her figure and her colouring? Guilt gnawed at him—it seemed to lie just below the surface and bubbled up at the slightest provocation. *Can I ever be free from it?*

Pushing the memory from his mind, he refocused on Chrissie. She hesitated as she recognised him, then moved slowly forward. Her usually radiant face was drawn and she looked unsure of herself. *What should I say? What if she runs?* As she drew nearer, he could see her eyes were glistening with tears.

"Chrissie, please, I had to see you."

"Tommy, you know we're not meant to meet. My parents won't allow it."

"Chrissie, your parents don't own you. Stand up to them for what you know is right. You should be free to do whatever you please."

"You don't understand. I owe them—they're so good to me, to Andy and me."

"Is this my son?" He looked into the pram. There were no words to describe the mix of emotions that fizzed through him, and he forgot his troubles. Completely overcome, his eyes glazed over as he reached out to touch the sleeping child. Andy's head was barely visible under a little cotton hat with images of Peter Rabbit and friends. "He's a bonnie wee chap," he whispered. "Can I hold him?"

"Not here, Tommy. Not where Mum might see."

"Where can we go? Chrissie, we need to talk."

"Tomorrow. I promise to meet you tomorrow. There's a little tea shop just down on the High Road. I'll meet you there at ten tomorrow morning." Chrissie looked back at her house, "I'd better go."

"Aye, tomorrow at ten then. I'll be waiting." Tommy gently patted his son's head and wished he could take them both home with him. "I miss you Chrissie."

Having seen Chrissie and Andy, Tommy's spirits lifted for the first time in months. A glimmer of hope surfaced, forcing the anxiety that had become his constant companion to lessen its grip. He made his way to the tube station and back to Dobbo's flat, where Tommy was dossing on the couch.

*

When he got to the flat he found Dobbo was home and in the kitchen.

"Beer?" Dobbo asked. His large bear-like body perched at a table etched with the graffiti of bored flatmates.

"Aye." Tommy pulled up a chair. "You wouldn't have a fag would you? I'm all out, and I'm skint."

Dobbo threw a pack of fags at him. "You need a job." He looked serious, in stark contrast to his usual countenance of the good-natured barman who spent his living pulling pints at the Jolly Miller.

"Aye, I do that." Tommy grimaced.

"How long do you think you'll be sticking around this time?"

"Depends, but I can't go home for a while."

"Hey, remember Nick from our Navy days? I hear he has a mate with a minicab who's looking for someone to drive some shifts for him. You interested?"

"Sure, but it'd be a joke trying to navigate my way round London."

"I reckon there's nothing to it. Just study the A-Z. I'll get Nick to give you his number—it'd be worth having a chat." Dobbo passed Tommy a beer.

"Cheers." Tommy took a sip. "I saw Chrissie today."

"Good for you. You guys getting back together?"

"I wish, but we're meeting up tomorrow to have a chat. Her parents still hate me. Saw my little man though—you should see him, so bonnie."

"He must've got that from Chrissie."

"Too right he did," Tommy laughed.

They sat in silence for a while and Tommy contemplated his situation. "Dobbo, it's good o' you to help me out like this. I'll get things sorted soon."

"Hey Tommy, we're like brothers. We've been through a lot together. I know you'd do the same for me."

"Aye, I would that. You sure your flatmates don't mind?" Tommy looked around the tatty kitchen with dishes piled up in the sink and discarded empty fish and chip wrappers littering the bench. Jerome and Ken, the other flatmates, were hardly ever home.

"No, why would they? It's good to be able to help you out."

Time to change the subject. "Ever think about the times aboard ship?" Tommy asked.

"Yeah, they were good and bad times. You were treated like scum by that petty officer—what's his name?"

"Ol' Cutlass? His real name was Petty Officer Collins, wasn't it?"

"That's the one. He sure picked on you. And he could get away with it." Dobbo chuckled. "Yep, we're better off here."

"The *Rusty B* weren't so bad, though it's no wonder she weren't the Navy's flagship."

Dobbo chuckled again. "Here's to you, able-bloody-seaman Stewart." Dobbo raised his glass in salute then emptied it in one long draught.

"Able-bloody-seaman Dobson, I salute you." Following suit, Tommy sculled his beer.

Dobbo reached for his glass and poured another. "Remember that time we had the force ten storm on our way back from the Caribbean? About two days out from Plymouth? Man, we took a pounding."

"Strewth, it was tough out on deck—those waves were even washing the bridge. She was rolling about, alright. I thought I was going to be a goner when I had to lash those lines."

"Yep, she was scary alright."

They sat in comfortable silence for a while. Life aboard ship had been hard, and Tommy had been targeted by bullies for being small and being a Scot. Ol' Cutlass was one of the worst. He had a mean streak and picked on Tommy endlessly, calling him girls' names, accusing him of not carrying out his duties, and disciplining him even when he hadn't done anything wrong. It was humiliating just thinking about it.

"It sure was tough. A man had to learn to fight back pretty fast." Tommy had struggled to fight back at first and he blamed his dad for that, but he'd learned to stand up for himself and the harassment seemed to stop as the bullies went after easier targets.

"The traditions are bad enough. It makes it easy for someone like Ol' Cutlass to move from harmless pranks to vindictive bullying. Navy ways suited him," Dobbo said.

"Aye. Some of the others were just as bad. Those bastards made my first year hell. Remember when they trashed my bedding? And worse was the night they soaked it."

"Yep, they trashed mine as well—only once, though. I made sure o' that. I landed that mongrel Smithy a good one—he was a bully. He needed to be taught a lesson. Bloody lucky I wasn't caught." Dobbo paused. "I wouldn't be going back, that's for sure."

"Aye, there's no going back."

Dobbo had been a good mate—a protector and an encourager. Tommy sure owed him.

At that moment the door opened and Ken, one of the flatmates, walked in. "You still here?" The greeting was hardly friendly.

"Aye, be here a bit longer if that's alright. Just getting sorted with my girl." Tommy shifted uneasily under Ken's hostile stare. "I don't suppose yer mind me dossing on the couch for a bit?".

Ignoring him, Ken opened the fridge door. "What's to eat round here?"

"Not a lot. We could do with a trip to the shops. Thought I might head down in the morning," Dobbo said.

Ken looked at Tommy, his dark complexion seeming to get darker. "We'll all need to put into the flat kitty, equal shares."

Tommy glanced at Dobbo.

"It's okay Ken, I'll take care of my mate here until he gets on his feet. He'll be getting a job and moving in with his girl any time now." Dobbo's voice was calming.

"Well this aint no charity lodging." Ken glared at Tommy.

It was too much. "Ach, give a man a break. I'm no bludger if that's what you mean. I'm down on me luck and need a few days, that's all." Tommy eyed Ken. "Aye, 'til my job starts."

"What's the job?" There was a hint of cynicism in his voice.

"It's nought to do with you." The words flashed out and Tommy stood to face Ken, his right fist clenched.

"Easy does it." Dobbo stood and put a hand on Tommy's arm, then turned from Tommy to Ken. "Like I said, I'll loan my mate here some money 'til he gets on his feet. And I expect that'll be soon enough. In the meantime, let's cool it and have us a beer."

"No thanks," Ken said looking at Tommy. "I'm going out."

"Tommy's a good mate, Ken—you'd do the same if it was one of your mates," Dobbo said, sitting back down.

Tommy let his shoulders drop and his hand relaxed.

Ken nodded at Dobbo. "Yeah, I guess you're right. I might see you down the Jolly later."

Tommy watched Ken's slightly overweight body head back out into the hall. The door closed with a bang.

"He's lucky I didn't deck him." Tommy emptied his glass.

"Cripes, then you'd have been out on your ear and I wouldn't have been able to help. No, there's no need for that—everything'll turn out okay. You'll see." Dobbo offered him a fag. "Chrissie will take you back. And driving's a great job."

Dobbo was right. Everything was going to turn out just fine.

*

Although Tommy was still haunted by the memory of that New Zealand woman, things were finally looking up. The sun was shining and the day was full of promise. He carried a London A-Z map book under his arm, which he'd been studying in preparation for the job interview with Nick's mate. And to top it off, he was about to meet Chrissie. They'd soon be together like a proper family.

With a spring in his step, Tommy made his way out of the tube station. People bustled about the High Road, enjoying the spell of good weather. He was swept along by the throng as he looked for the tea shop Chrissie had mentioned. There it was. He raked his hand through his hair and tried to calm his mounting excitement, before weaving through the crowd towards the shop. Once inside, he looked for Chrissie. No sign of her. His watch showed he was a few minutes early, and he sat down to wait at a table in the corner.

The tea shop was a crowded noisy place with a dozen or more small round wooden tables with rickety chairs. Chatter reverberated through the room and the regular ring of the cash register added to the clatter. The counter had a lip-smacking selection of savouries, sandwiches, slices and cakes. Brewed coffee provided a welcoming aroma. The walls were littered with magazine pin-ups of the royal couple, Charles and Diana. They seemed to be everywhere these days. The newspaper agents and shop windows were full of their pictures, fuelling the public's current feeding frenzy.

The sound of the door opening caught his attention and he looked up to see Chrissie. Spotting Andy wasn't with her, Tommy deflated, then pulled himself up to sit erect as his disappointment flared. *How dare she not bring my own flesh and blood to see me?*

Spotting him, Chrissie came over to the table and sat down.

He glared at her. "Where's Andy?"

"I thought it best to leave him with Mum—he's teething and he's a bit grizzly." Chrissie placed her bag on the spare seat. "Do you want a drink?"

Bristling, his anger seemed to take on a life of its own as it boiled over and he just couldn't stop himself. "You've no right to keep Andy from me. He's bloody well mine as well! I've more right to him than your stupid cow of a mother. Strewth, Chrissie, can't you understand that?"

"No. How dare you!" Chrissie looked stunned.

"You were always too stupid to see that your precious mother and father control you like a puppet on a bloody string." His voice was getting louder and louder. He had to make her understand. "You dance to their tune and don't give a toss about the people who should really matter to you."

His words bounced off the painted walls. Chrissie glared at him and he knew his words had found their target.

"Tommy, don't." It was a warning. "I came here to talk to you, but if you're going to act like a bully, then I'm not going to waste my time." Her chair scraped across the tiled floor as she stood up, swinging her bag over her shoulder.

Seeing the glances from other customers, Tommy lowered his voice. "Wait, I'm sorry. Chrissie, please don't go. We need to talk."

Still glowering, Chrissie slipped back onto the chair. "One more chance, Tommy Stewart. But I'm warning you, I don't need to do this."

"I miss you and I want you back. Please Chrissie, I can make you happy. Just give me a chance." He could lose her forever, and he didn't want that.

"You've had your chances. You always mess up. I trusted you and you hit me. How can I be sure you won't hit Andy? You've a right temper and you're out of control too often. I have to protect my son."

Tension built as they sat in an uneasy silence for a few minutes, his gut turning somersaults. He'd done it again—lost his temper in an instant, and now he had to patch things up. *What an idiot.*

Chrissie finally broke the silence. "Did you want a drink?"

"Nay, I'm skint. I'm soon to get a job, though."

"Really? That's good news. I'm going to get a cuppa." She stood up, not even waiting to hear what the job was.

Doesn't she care?

Chrissie went over to the counter and ordered. The tray she brought back had a teapot, milk jug, and two cups and saucers.

"Now, tell me about the job?"

"It's a cabbie, here in London."

"I thought you had to sit some big test about the streets around London, and that it takes years to get a licence?"

"Nay, I'll be driving a minicab. The test you're talking about is The Knowledge. It's only for the black-cab drivers. Anyone can drive a minicab. Remember Dobbo's mate Nick?" He paused and waited for Chrissie's nod before continuing. "He happens to have a friend who owns a minicab and I'm driving a shift for him."

"Really? That's a bit of luck."

Seizing the opportunity, he added, "See, I'll be able to look after you and the bairn. I'll get a place and we can move in together. Aye, we'll be a real family—just you, me and our wee bairn."

Chrissie took her time in setting out the cups on their saucers and pouring milk into the bottom of each before pouring the tea. Passing one to him, she held his gaze for a moment. "Tommy, it's not going to work. We both know it won't. And we have to do what's best for Andy. I can't risk it—he's too precious. You have to learn to control your anger. You have to grow up before you can take responsibility for a family. I'm sorry."

His shoulders slumped as his world crumbled. *How can I live without Chrissie?* His breathing became shallow as if he was crushed by a heavy weight and he felt the sweat gather under his arms then along his spine. *How can I no' see my boy growing up?*

"Chrissie, please hear me out. I promise I'll be a good father. Just give me a chance. I wanna see Andy take his first steps—to walk and run. I wanna hear him say his first words, to call me Da'. I wanna teach him to kick a ball and ride a bike and to do all that stuff that kids do. My own da' bullied me, but I wanna protect Andy and be there for him." Taking a risk, he reached out and took her hand in his. "I love you, Chrissie. Aye, we're meant to be together. You'll see."

Chrissie looked confused and pulled her hand away. "Tommy, please don't. You're making this hard for me. I care for you, but things are different now and I have to put Andy first."

Vaguely aware that Chrissie was continuing to speak, Tommy found himself studying her neck. He'd always been attracted to her long slender neck, but then he imagined his hands around it, hurting her.

No. I can't, I won't!

He tried to get the thought out of his head, but his mind was filled with an image of the New Zealand girl, those piercing blue eyes pleading with him to stop. It was like he was playing God, having power over life. Not a feeling he'd had before.

That girl would have done anything to stop me hurting her.

If only he had power over Chrissie, like he'd had over the girl on the track. Then they'd get on with their lives, together. The sense of power was almost intoxicating.

No, I have to stop!

"Tommy, are you hearing me?" Chrissie interrupted with a note of frustration in her voice.

"Aye. What was it you were saying?" *Pull yourself together!*

"I said I think we should test things out for a few months. Maybe we should meet like this once a week for a while, and I'll bring Andy next time. Once you start working, we can see how you get on. No promises, though. And I'll have to handle my parents."

"Ach, I want more. I want us to get back together. Hell, I know we can make it work." He slowly turned the cup in its saucer. His voice now resigned, he said, "But if that's as far as you're prepared to go for now, then I guess that's it."

He retreated back into silence and sulked as he finished his tea. He would have to be patient.

7

Three days after leaving Largs, Rose was back in London and walking down Totteridge Lane to the doctor's surgery, on the orders of Mrs Cohen. The older woman had been appalled by her injuries and tale of woe. She insisted Rose visit the doctor to get her injuries checked out.

Her senses were on red alert and she started at the sound of a twig breaking behind her. Was someone following her? She twisted her stiff neck and shoulders to glance around, fearing the worst. A man was approaching, catching her up. Terror, now all too familiar, crept up her spine and dampness spread profusely across her skin and she shivered with chill even though it was a warm summer's morning.

Picking up her pace, she tried to out-stride him. The path ahead veered away from the road and went through a grove of small trees before returning to the kerbside. A steady stream of cars made their way towards the High Road, caught in the morning rush. Their noise was both disturbing and comforting. Apprehensive, she sensed the strangers within were watching her, yet at the same time they offered her protection.

Should she stick to the path or walk along the kerbside? Nausea rose from the pit of her stomach and she could taste the bile in her mouth. She swallowed hard, which pained her swollen throat. Would she make it to the doctor's surgery? Looking over her shoulder again, the man had gained ground and was about to overtake her. She gripped her bag and realised she had no means of defending herself, other than her own strength and cunning.

"Morning," the stranger said as he passed.

"M... morning." And then he was ahead of her, posing no threat. She had to get a grip on her fear, but it was only a few days since her ordeal and she was struggling to contain her emotions.

Rose glanced behind her again, but no one was there. If only she'd stayed in the safety of the house. She wasn't even sure what the doctor could do.

The sign advertising the surgery was now visible. Relieved, she quickly walked the last hundred metres or so.

Inside, she gave her name to the receptionist and slipped into the surgery waiting room. Others were waiting and she sensed their discreet glances. She knew her bloated and bruised neck, black eyes and fat lips looked grotesque. *If only I'd stayed home.*

As a distraction, she forced herself to study her surroundings. The doctor's surgery was part of what would once have been yet another mansion on Totteridge Lane. The waiting room had lavish wooden panels and a high ceiling. The windows looked out onto a typical manicured English garden. The seats were comfortable leather and an array of *Country Life, Discover Britain* and *Vanity Fair* magazines littered the table in the centre. A crystal chandelier hung from the high vaulted wooden ceiling above.

She picked up a *Country Life* magazine and flicked the pages, barely taking in its contents. Her eyes darted around the room, and she felt self-conscious among the twinsets and pearls.

"Rose Wells?" The words came from a short silver-haired man who Rose guessed was in his mid-fifties. The doctor, she presumed.

"Yes, that's me." She followed the doctor into an office, where he motioned her to sit in the chair on the other side of a large leather and mahogany desk.

"Rose, I'm Doctor Hubbard. Now, how can I help you?" His cultured English accent matched his navy pinstripe suit, complete with a folded handkerchief in his breast pocket.

"I'm not sure if there's anything you can do to help. I was in Scotland last week, and a stranger attacked me and tried to strangle me. Mrs Cohen thought I should get you to look over my injuries, just in case."

"Let's take a look then." Dr Hubbard peered over his glasses before moving around the desk to sit beside her. "Ah, it looks to me like you have had quite a nasty experience. Can you tell me how it happened?"

Rose briefly recounted her story as the doctor examined her injuries. His gentle manner and sympathetic responses triggered another bout of tears. The next thing she knew, she was sobbing with her face buried in his chest, his fine woollen suit absorbing her tears.

"A-hem!" he cleared his throat.

Embarrassed, she sat up and tried to pull herself together. He passed her the linen hanky from his pocket. As she dabbed, she could see his discomfort and she almost wanted to laugh. Her outburst was totally opposite to the stereotypical British 'stiff upper lip'. He moved away, back to the safety of the far side of his desk.

"Rose, your injuries are healing nicely and there's no sign of infection. I can't see any underlying issues that we need to be concerned about. Your movements are all good, although the bruising will take some time to diminish. But I don't see any major problems. I'll get the nurse to re-dress the wounds on your neck and head."

"Thanks, doctor."

"You are a lucky young woman to have come out of this assault so well. You could easily have lost consciousness, either when you sustained those high impact injuries to your head or when you were struggling for oxygen." He scribbled something on his pad.

"I guess my guardian angel was looking out for me."

"Quite so. If you don't mind, I would like to photograph your injuries to keep as a record. I have an application form here for compensation through a government run scheme called 'Victims of Violence'. This scheme targets victims of violent acts who are unable to get compensation through the courts. If you are agreeable, I can fill it out and I suggest you sign it. What do you think?"

"I'd appreciate that. Thanks, Doctor."

"How do you feel about seeing a trauma counsellor?"

"No, thanks. I'm okay. I'll sort myself out." That would just mean more excursions out of the house.

"Rose, did you ever fall off a horse or a bicycle and have someone say to you the best thing was to get straight back on and try again?"

"Sure."

"Well, a word of advice—this is a bit like that. You need to try and get back to normal as quickly as you can. Do the things you did before the assault. Carry on with living life like you did before. I know that you must feel changed by it, but your normal activities will help you to recover faster."

"I am trying, but it's hard." She made a silent vow to try harder.

"Then I'll ask the nurse to dress the wounds and I will leave the form at reception for you to sign. Good day, Rose."

*

"Rose, I came as soon as I could. How're you feeling?" Kathy stood at the door, a broad grin lighting up a face perfectly framed by blonde curls.

"I'm okay. There was no need to come round, but it's good to see you," Rose said. "Come on in."

Kathy came inside and Rose shut and bolted the door before leading her through to the morning room. She loved this bright and airy room with its panels of long narrow windows looking out over the garden, its wallpaper covered in small sprigs of flowers.

"Cripes, your face and neck are sure a mess. I couldn't believe it when I heard—Mrs Cohen rang and told Stephanie, who rang me."

"Yeah, it's been a bit of a shock—sure knocks your confidence."

"Have the cops found him yet?" asked Kathy.

Rose tried to keep the tremor from her voice. "I don't think so. At least, I haven't heard." That she hadn't heard from them angered her. It was as if they were ignoring her case like it wasn't important. Quick to change the subject, she asked, "Do you wanna drink? The coffee's fresh."

"Sure, thanks."

Going across to the kitchen, she poured two mugs of coffee and came back and handed one to Kathy.

"Cheers." Kathy lifted her mug up in a mock toast. "So what happened exactly?"

Although telling only a brief version of her story, the tears flowed and Rose held her coffee mug with trembling hands, sipping as she talked. She tried to imagine she was just recounting someone else's story, but she was still full of fear.

Kathy moved closer and put her arm around her. "I'm sorry, Rose. Is there anything I can do to help?"

Moved by her compassion, the sobs began afresh. "No—thanks. I just have to get over it. One minute I'm angry and the next I'm afraid. So much has changed, and all because of one stupid event."

"I can't begin to imagine what it must be like. Poor you." Kathy looked genuinely mortified.

Rose cradled her coffee mug in both hands. "Yeah, I feel violated—as if I'm not safe in my own skin. I'm so angry that I'm a victim because I'm a woman—I bet it wouldn't happen to a man. I'm angry at him for what he's done. But at the same time, I actually feel sorry for him—I don't think he knew what he was doing."

"We're all responsible for our own actions. It makes me sick to think there are predators like him out there," Kathy said.

"Rose," Daniel called in his childish voice. "Rose!"

"In here, Daniel," she called back.

Her three-year-old charge came running into the room, his cheeky ear-to-ear grin exposing a dimple in one cheek. His dark eyes were wide and his thick brown hair looked like he'd been in his makeshift hut of blankets and cushions. "Rose, can you play with me?" Seeing her, he climbed onto her lap and put his little arms around her in a hug. Pulling back, he reached out and traced her tears with his finger. "Don't cry."

Rose and Kathy both laughed.

"It's okay, Daniel. I'm all better now." She kissed him on the cheek.

"I love you, Rose." His serious tone matched his serious expression.

"And I love you." She looked back at Kathy. "Being here has really helped. Mrs Cohen is so supportive and I love looking after Daniel. He's such a welcome distraction and I love his innocence. He's a constant reminder of how much I have to look forward to."

Kathy chatted some more, bringing her up to speed with what the girls had been up to. Rose felt her spirits lift.

"I'd best get going." Kathy got up and went over to the kitchen to put her cup on the bench.

"Yeah, I'd better get back to work, but I'll see you out first. And thanks for coming Kathy, I really appreciate it." Hand-in-hand with Daniel, she walked her friend to the door.

*

It was several days since Kathy's visit and Rose hadn't been out of the house, despite the beautiful summer days and garden full of flowers. Mrs Cohen had taken Daniel to an appointment and the housework was finished for the day, which meant Rose had some free time before she needed to start the evening meal. Even though she'd locked all the doors and windows after Mrs Cohen left, she'd been around twice more since to check they were all safely secured.

More than a week had passed since the assault and she'd still been unable to write home. She couldn't tell her parents—they'd only worry. She'd grown up in a loving home in conservative, rural New Zealand. All her life she'd been sheltered from violence, making her unprepared for dealing with it now. But if her parents knew, they would be distraught and maybe even fly across to London—and that wasn't necessary. Or else they'd want her to go home, but she wasn't ready to leave. She'd wanted to share the trauma with Gary, but it had been too difficult to put it on paper.

With the house quiet, she went into her room and sat at her desk. The room was small and drab, in contrast to the rest of the house. The walls were plain cream, brightened with photos of Gary and her family. The furniture was minimalist, a single bed with a dull floral cover, a bedside table, a small desk, a wardrobe. The bowl of granny smith apples was a reminder that she was the hired help—so different to the large bowl of forbidden exotic fruits downstairs.

Through the small window she could see the beautiful tree-lined garden. She looked longingly at the swimming pool, with its stylish landscaping and Mediterranean ceramics. Today was hot and she'd love a swim, but John the gardener didn't appear to be around and she was too scared to venture out into the garden without the security of having him there.

Gary. If only you were here.

She opened the drawer and pulled out a blank sheet of paper. She stared at it while chewing the end of her pen, then looked up and saw Gary grinning from the photograph on the wall. That did it. She began to write. It was hard at first, but then the words flowed and sharing her story with him was comforting. She carefully folded the letter and placed it in an envelope to post.

Now what? Rose paced the house in frustration, listless and bored with reading and being on her own. It was like being in a cage. She decided to call Kathy.

"Rose, it's good to hear from you," Kathy said in her thick Aussie accent. "I was going to ring you. I have the house to myself next Saturday and I'm thinking of getting the girls together. I'm hoping you can come. I know it's early days for you after your ordeal, but it'll do you good to get out again."

"I don't know, Kathy. I'm not sure I'm ready for it."

"You need to try, Rose. We'll just be at home having a meal, a few drinks and a video. We've just got a copy of *Les Misérables*, an old black and white film from the 1930's. I thought it'd be fun to watch that."

"I'll think about it."

"Okay. But try and make it. It's our last chance to see Carmen before she goes home."

"I'll let you know. But I'd have to take the bus ..."

"So how's it going?"

"Alright I suppose. It just takes time. I haven't got the confidence to go out into the garden yet, unless someone I can trust is about. You know, I wish it had happened at night. Then I'd only be afraid in the dark. But because it was daytime, I can't seem to shake it off no matter what time it is."

The doorbell rang and Rose muttered under her breath, "Oh no."

"You alright, Rose?" Kathy sounded concerned.

"It's the doorbell. Can you stay on the line, just in case?"

"Sure. But please be quick—I should be working."

Rose left the phone and went to the door. Making sure the chain was across, she unlocked it and opened it a crack. It was only Bill, the interior decorator. Relieved, she slipped the chain off and opened the door. He was wearing white overalls and carried a large paint tin with a brush and roller.

"Hi, Bill. Come on in." She gave him a beaming smile.

Tall and thin, he walked with a stoop, exposing even more of his balding hair and he grinned back at her, looking more like a comedian. "'Allo, Rose. How're you doing?" It was easy to detect his cockney roots.

"Not too bad, I guess. Just a minute, I'm on the phone."

Going back to the phone, she picked up the receiver. "It was only Bill coming round to do some more work on the house. I'll give Saturday some thought."

"Sure, see you then, I hope. Bye."

"Bye, and thanks," she said as she replaced the receiver in its cradle.

Bill popped his head into the kitchen. "Did they catch the geezer?"

"No, I don't think so."

"Are you getting better then?"

"Yeah, I guess so. But I'm still too scared to go out."

"Why don't you carry some weapons? You know, like mace or a pepper spray? Or even a truncheon? It might help build up your confidence."

"Maybe you're right."

"Tell you what. If you have a soft bag, I can fashion a club out of a piece of hardwood. I'll make sure it has sharp corners and you can carry it in your bag—it'll still do some damage even without pulling it out."

"Do you really think so? Thanks, Bill. I guess I could use one. I have a soft bag I can use."

"I don't think it's legal to carry pepper spray. But you can put a pepper pot in your bag and it only takes a second to remove the top and throw it in some poor geezer's face."

"Yeah, I guess that could work." Although doubtful about using a weapon, she allowed Bill's enthusiasm to boost her confidence. He was the tonic she needed and, for the first time in over a week, she hoped she might be able to overcome her fear.

*

It was still daylight when Rose, drawing on all her courage, stepped out of the driveway and onto the street. She moved with trepidation, clutching the soft suede bag that concealed her newly acquired pepper pot and the piece of hardwood Bill had fashioned into a weapon. She paused and lit a cigarette. It wasn't that she wanted to smoke, but the glowing tip provided her with another weapon.

She crossed the road and walked the half mile to the bus stop. Outwardly, she tried to portray her usual calm, but inwardly she was a mess. Memories hounded her and she imagined danger in every shadow, in every bush. It was as if the cars carried faceless assailants and the pedestrians were all predators. She debated whether she should turn back.

At the bus stop, she stood next to the shelter and waited. She drew on the smoke, just enough to keep it glowing. Buses were rarely on schedule making her feel vulnerable as she waited. Alone.

Silently, she urged the bus to be on time. To help stay calm, she counted the cars as they passed.

A man walked towards her and she gripped her bag tighter. He seemed to be unnecessarily studying her. But as he reached the bus stop, he nodded to her and put his briefcase down. She looked down and, seeing her knuckle was white, eased her grip a little and finished the cigarette.

A diesel motor sounded in the distance and a bus came ambling towards her. Sighing deeply to relieve her mounting tension, she boarded the bus. After handing over her coins, she moved down the aisle to a seat at the back where she could watch the other passengers.

The trip passed swiftly and she was soon disembarking and heading into Kathy's house.

"Come in, Rose. It's great to see you." Kathy thrust a glass at her and added, "Here, have a glass of champers."

"Thanks, it's good to be out." She stepped inside the grandiose marble entrance hall with the spiralling staircase and spectacular chandeliers. "Every time I see this place I'm grateful I don't have to clean it," she said.

"Tell me about it. Come on through to the party—everyone's here already."

Fleetwood Mac was playing loudly on the stereo and Stephanie, Carmen, Susan, Ute, Jane and a couple of girls Rose didn't recognise were dancing in the spacious lounge.

Carmen came over and kissed her on both cheeks. "'Allo, Rose. Poor you. So sorry when I hear what happen to you." The German girl pronounced the words slowly with her strong accent.

"Thanks, but I'm okay now."

"So glad you come. I didn't want to miss you." Carmen frowned as she looked at Rose's neck. "Does it still make pain?"

"The sores are a lot better already."

"Does this mean you won't come and visit me now?"

"No way. I wouldn't miss it for the world. I can't wait to see some of Europe and you'll be my first priority."

"That is so good. I love that you come."

The others came over and crowded Rose, hugging her gently. They took an interest in her wounds, which were still prominent, although the swelling had gone down. Eager to get back to the dancing, they didn't overly dwell on it. The girls were on form and Rose loved being back with them. The laughter and good-natured banter wiped away her angst and she was able to relax.

Kathy called them through to the separate dining room, its space filled with a large dining table surrounded by carved mahogany chairs. Places had been set and platters of cold meats, salads and sweet treats filled its surface.

"Find a seat everyone," Kathy said, while drawing the plush burgundy velvet curtains across the windows along one wall.

"Wow, Kathy. This spread's amazing!" A chorus of endorsements followed.

"I think I'll take this one," Jane said in her thick Aussie accent and pulled out an elaborate chair at the head of the table that could have doubled for a throne.

"Trust you," Kathy said.

Rose chose a seat further down the table from Jane, who could be overbearing and obnoxious at times. It was best to avoid her company.

"Okay everyone, dig in," Kathy said once all nine were seated.

"Crumbs, we could've gone down to the local and put out an open invite—this table's enormous," Susan, one of the new girls, said.

Kathy giggled. "Can you imagine the family eating here? There's only the four of them."

"You're kidding. Do they use this room daily or just when they have guests?"

"Daily. It's a bit upstairs downstairs, 'cos I have to wait on them." Kathy passed a platter around.

The ostentatious room matched the rest of the house. Mahogany sideboards showed off silver candelabra and great silver serving dishes, under several large oil paintings in ornate frames.

"How did they make their money?" Jane asked, helping herself to a generous serving of meats.

"He has a business selling nuclear fallout shelters—there's one under the backyard, complete with emergency food and water." Winking at Rose, Kathy added, "Rose and I took a look one time and you'd be amazed at the stuff down there. We found a whole stash of chocolates—they may find a few missing from the carton if they ever have to live in the shelter."

"And people buy those shelters?" Steph asked.

"Yep. I think it's a bit of a joke," Kathy replied. "But there's obviously a market 'cos they get their millions from somewhere. The fear factor is pretty strong."

"That's for sure," Rose said, thinking about her own fears.

"What sort of person buys a nuclear fallout shelter for their backyard?" Steph asked before adding, "Other than moles, that is."

"Those who have too much money and nothing better to spend it on," Jane said.

"They're part of the nouveau riche class who like to flaunt their wealth, but they don't have the style and class like the old wealthy families—everything's just a little bit tacky," Kathy said. "How about a game of Truth?"

"How do you play that game?" Ute asked.

"We go round the table and each person gets to say something about themselves that's true and hard to guess, and two things that are false. We have to choose which is true."

"Great idea," Rose said, wanting to get into the spirit of things.

"Okay, you start. What're your three things?" Kathy asked.

"Let me see." Rose took her time before answering. "I sky-dived for my eighteenth birthday, met Gary on a blind date or got a lift hitchhiking with a biker gang. Which one's true?"

"That's easy," Steph said. "It'll be the Gary one." The girls laughed.

"Close, but wrong. It was the hitchhiking with the biker gang."

"Really? Were you scared?" Kathy asked.

"Sure was—or at least I thought I was." Lesmahagow had given her a new standard for scared.

"How did you meet Gary?" Carmen asked.

"A mutual friend tried to hook us up on a blind date, but I refused. After all, what sort of a loser goes on a blind date?"

"So true!" Steph laughed.

Rose chuckled. "I went along with another friend—just as a partner, nothing more. By the time he arrived to pick me up, he'd already had a few too many beers and I ditched him soon after we got to the cabaret. I joined my friend's table, and was introduced to Gary. We danced together for the rest of the evening."

"Nice," Susan said. "Now it's my turn ..."

The other girls took their turns at Truth and laughed at the outrageous things they'd either done or not done. The noise level increased as the drinks flowed and the girls then chattered and joked about the interesting and sometimes strange goings-on in their employers' households.

Jane turned to Rose. "Rose, why didn't you press charges?"

The room went quiet as all eyes turned to Rose. It was an unwelcome change in topic and Rose shifted in her chair, annoyance destroying her earlier peace. "I was advised not to. The cops will get him the help he needs without me pressing charges and going through the courts." Her response was measured and flat.

"But what if he does it again? You'll be guilty for not stopping him. If he kills someone, you'll have blood on your hands too. You might as well strangle her yourself."

"How can you say that?" Rose was angry now. "You've absolutely no idea what sort of hell I've been going through. I trust the cops to do their job and make sure he doesn't do it again. If I need your advice, I'll ask for it."

"I'm just saying I think you're wrong not doing anything," Jane said.

"Jane, that's a bit rough," Kathy shifted uncomfortably in her chair.

"Well, it's true."

"No, it's not. Rose can't be held responsible for his actions. You need to shut your mouth." Relieving the tension, Kathy added, "C'mon, let's go through and watch the video."

No more was said on the subject and Rose tried to hide how much it had upset her as they settled in to watch *Les Misérables*. She became so engrossed in the story that she barely noticed the time. The revolution was just beginning when she looked at her watch and saw the last bus was about to leave.

Grabbing her jacket and bag, she garbled her farewells and scrambled out the door. It was now dark. Very dark. She was the only one of her friends living in Totteridge and the only one to take the bus. Alone and feeling vulnerable, her fear grew and the night's darkness made it ten times worse. Her stomach tightened and nausea replaced the earlier satiated feeling she'd been enjoying. Moisture pricked at her spine. Steeped in fear, she hurried to the bus stop, gripping the hardwood in the bag.

The bus arrived on time and Rose had to sprint the last few metres to catch it. Again she sat in the back row so she could watch the other passengers. The evening had been loads of fun and she was glad she'd made the effort to go. She was sick and tired of being on her own and missed having the freedom to socialise with her friends—she loved being with the girls.

But she was scared, so very scared.

Damn him! If I don't deal to my fear, I'm in danger of becoming a fruitcake for the rest of my life. It's not fair. I want my OE and I want to see Europe, especially now I've come this far. She stared out at the darkness. *How can I stop becoming a complete nutter? It's endless—he keeps on hurting me. It's like he has power over me, even now it's supposedly over. And it's going to keep on going for as long as I live in fear.*

The bus pulled into her stop and Rose disembarked. She lit a cigarette, holding it at the ready, and gripped the hardwood in the bag. As she walked a slight noise behind caused her to turn, but she could see only shadows.

Shadows.

Walking along under the streetlights she watched how her shadow changed. She could use the shadows. Approaching the streetlight, the shadow lay behind her and slowly shortened until she was directly under the light. And then it moved in front of her, lengthening as she moved away. Between the lights, multiple shadows crossed from the light behind, the light ahead and those across the street. Testing her theory, she found there was only a short length where she wouldn't be able to detect a movement behind her. It was unlikely that someone could come at her from behind without her knowing, so she strode forward with a dash more confidence.

Damn it, I refuse to become a victim. I need to focus on the positives—there must be some good that has come out of this mess.

Inspired now, it was like a cloud had moved to allow the moon to light up the darkness.

But what could possibly be positive about almost being strangled?

Running her hand through her hair, she struggled with this new line of thought.

Well, I guess I've learned to trust myself when truly terrified. How many people are lucky enough to have confidence in that? And I know I'll do the right thing in a real crisis—that's a positive. I know I tend to suffer delayed shock, which gives me time to think and act—I could have been killed if shock had paralysed me. How many people get to find that out about themselves? How many live to tell the story?

Now she felt more self-assured.

Hey, I'm alive and that's pretty positive. In fact, I'm lucky. No, I'm damned lucky. What are the chances of surviving an assault like that? And what are the chances of it ever happening again? I bet they're long odds for it to happen twice in a lifetime. And if the odds are long, then I'm safer now than before.

Sure, she knew this logic was flawed, but it didn't matter. She was on a roll and could feel her boldness mounting with every heartbeat.

There's a lot to be thankful for and I've a lot to live for. I need to get on with my life and stop being such a wimp. He's not going to get the better of me.

Feeling resolute about this new mindset, Rose walked the remaining half mile from the bus stop with a spring in her step.

*

Two weeks later, Rose stepped out from the central London café, her spirit light from enjoying a meal with Kathy and Sue. Unfazed by the pelting rain, she stood looking for a cab. Normally, she'd opt to walk to Leicester Square to catch the tube home, but rather than be drenched she decided to spend the money and take a cab. Unlike home, there were no verandas offering shelter from the rain, and she didn't have a brolly.

She'd resolved not to be afraid anymore and was becoming bolder by the day. She could do this. It was easy to be cynical about New Year's resolutions and she'd always been the first to laugh at friends who'd made them, only to break them within days. But this resolution was different. She needed to push through. Otherwise he'd won—and that wasn't an option. Time and determination were great healers—this she repeated like a mantra.

A taxi cruised into view. She waved it down. But it had a fare and sped on past. Next a minicab slowed and stopped fairly close to her from which a passenger got out. She made a dash for it and slipped into the back seat, saying, more as a question than an instruction, "Leicester Square?"

The cabbie mumbled something, his Scottish accent triggering a spasm in her gut. Paranoia threatened to overwhelm her, and she forced herself to relax.

What are the chances of being randomly assaulted twice in your lifetime?

It was a question she'd asked herself many times over the last few days. She'd chosen to believe the odds were long, and she'd continue to tell herself that. They protected her. And she was smarter and wiser for the experience.

It was a ten-minute ride to Leicester Square tube station and the cabbie remained uncharacteristically silent throughout the entire ride. She didn't mind, there was safety in the car. It gave her a chance to look around, enjoying watching the people with their colourful umbrellas darting about to avoid the puddles. In here, she didn't need to worry about who might be watching her.

Rain was still pelting down when they pulled into the taxi rank. After checking the meter, she counted out the exact change and handed it to the cabbie. For some reason, he kept his head down, refusing to meet her eyes. She stifled a giggle as she remembered one of her father's favourite sayings: *Strange, but there's none so queer as folk.* She climbed out of the cab and hurried into the tube station to avoid a drenching.

8

Tommy had been driving the minicab for just over four weeks and was at home behind the wheel, even though he was still getting his head around the labyrinth of London streets. Although it was a temporary arrangement, he was grateful to John, Nick's mate, who owned the minicab and had given him the break.

The minicab was based in Golders Green, the Jewish quarter in the north of London. Minicab jobs were mostly pre-booked and this worked well for him, as he could look up the directions before picking up the fare. But there had been a few times he'd had to stop and check the A to Z, annoying his punters. The shift work was hard to get used to, often starting early evening and going through to the wee hours, but the pay wasn't bad.

He'd just pulled up outside a Soho club and his passenger waved a twenty quid note at him.

"Keep the change," the punter said as he scrambled out of the cab and into the rain.

Tommy was about to set off again when he noticed a young woman in a black raincoat running towards him. She was holding a newspaper over her head in a futile attempt to thwart the rain. She made a hailing motion with the newspaper, before running the few strides across the pavement and opening his rear door.

"Leicester Square?" she asked by way of a request.

"Aye, hop in."

The door closed and he edged the cab out into the flow of traffic and settled into the steady pace set by the cars ahead. A glance in the rear vision mirror found him looking at a vaguely familiar face. He was back on that abandoned railway track with his hands around the throat of a young woman. Those deep blue eyes were looking at him, urging him to stop. Overwhelmed by guilt, his pulse raced and sweat stuck his shirt against the seat. If only he could hit the rewind button and undo that fateful day. The toot of a horn caught his attention and he cursed as he jammed on his brakes, prompting an audible intake of breath from the back seat.

He tried to keep his head down as he pulled up to the taxi rank outside Leicester Square Station, not wanting to be recognised. He took her money before moving back out into the traffic, ignoring any prospective punters.

The encounter left him feeling edgy, and he drove around for a few blocks without calling the controller, not wanting another fare. *What if it had been her? What if she recognised me?*

He could hear Dave, the controller, assigning pre-booked jobs over the radio. They were mostly short fares, deepening his bleak mood. The cream jobs went to the inner circle, those cabbies who liked to sit around the base playing cards and drinking. Those cabbies didn't spend half the time he did on the road, yet they made more money, because they scored the cushy numbers to places like the airports that guaranteed easy return fares. If he was going to provide for Chrissie and wee Andy, he'd have to stay on the right side of the controller.

Money was tight with a portion of his earnings going to John, the minicab owner, for the radio call sign and insurance. Needing fares to make money, he focused on finding his next one—he couldn't keep driving about the streets without the paying passengers.

A smartly dressed elderly couple were standing at a taxi rank and they motioned towards him. They looked like high rollers and he seized the opportunity. Dave had stressed that only the black cabs could use the ranks, but there were none in sight, so he took a punt and pulled up.

"The Roux at Parliament Square, Great George Street, and make it snappy." The man's dapper grey suit, white shirt and bow tie matched his cultured accent.

"Aye, take a seat."

The gentleman ushered the lady wearing a flowery flowing dress with hat into the cab. The door closed just as a black cab pulled up. The driver got out.

"Oi, get off our patch, yer useless git!"

Annoyed at being caught, Tommy manoeuvred the cab back into the traffic.

"I say, what was all that about?" asked the toff in the back seat.

"Nought," he said, unwilling to discuss the rules surrounding London cabbies. There were always rules. He'd been subjected to them by his da' and then again in the Navy. Being hamstrung by countless rules and regulations tended to bring out his rebellious nature, which nearly always ended in trouble.

"Outside your jurisdiction were you?" The very correct sounding voice responded from the backseat.

"Nay, never mind."

They lapsed into silence. He'd been warned there were severe penalties if you were caught with passengers who weren't pre-booked. Just last week, the cabbies were discussing how two black cab drivers had attacked a minicab driver caught poaching on their rank.

As he turned the cab into Charles II Street to avoid the congested Pall Mall and Trafalgar Square area, the man in the back spoke, "I say, why take this route? It would be shorter to go down Whitehall."

Peeved at this interruption, Tommy responded, "Trust me, this way's quicker."

"Preposterous, you cabbies are all the same—you think you can fleece your clients."

Tommy gritted his teeth and continued on his path. As expected, the traffic was flowing nicely. He intended to take The Mall into Horse Guards, and indicated accordingly.

"I say, you would be better to take Whitehall," the punter said from the back seat.

"Ach, it'll be too congested."

"Cabbies, they're a law unto themselves," the passenger muttered to the lady.

Tommy flicked off his indicator and continued towards Charing Cross and Whitehall. As expected, the traffic was heavy around Charing Cross and they were nose-to-tail along Whitehall. The meter ticked on and he was irritated.

Pulling up outside the restaurant, he couldn't resist. "Strewth, I drive these streets every day and I know the best route—that's why you pay me. When you go to the restaurant, do you go into the kitchen and instruct the chef on how to cook the meal?"

"Such impertinence." The man pulled the change out of his wallet without the customary tip.

Tommy was seething. He was fed up with toffs and hated being treated like he was worthless. Distracted, he pulled out into the traffic, cutting off a black cab and leaving it honking in his wake.

His night didn't get any better. A call came to pick someone up outside a bar in Hammersmith and deliver him to an address in Croydon. An intoxicated youth was waiting. Once in the back seat, he slumped over and appeared to fall asleep.

Arriving in Croydon, Tommy shook him and said, "Laddie, wake up, we're here."

The punter made a show of searching through his pockets and mumbled, "Seems I've misplaced my wallet. I've some money in my flat. Can you wait while I go get it?"

Tommy waited for a good ten minutes before realising the young man was a bilker—he'd scarpered. His composure lost, Tommy thumped on the horn and wove back into the traffic.

Bloody hell, it's no' my fault, but why does crap always happen to me?

His shift was coming to an end. After nearly twelve hours on the job, he headed back to base.

*

Ring—ring, ring—ring.
"Hello?"
"Ma, is that you?"

"Tommy. Awrite?"

"Aye, and you?"

"Aye, Tommy. Where're you calling from?"

"London. I'm lodging with Dobbo."

"Aye, I thought you'd be there. Tommy, the police came around looking for you. Sergeant Moffat."

The air seemed to leave his lungs and he paused to steady himself before asking, "When, Ma?"

"Ach, just after you left. Did you do something, son?"

"Nay, Ma. What did you tell him?" His pulse was racing and beads of sweat formed on his brow.

"What's there to tell? I said you're in London. He didn't seem too worried. I haven't heard from him since."

"Does Da' know?"

"Aye, he was home when the policeman came calling." She continued speaking before Tommy could respond. "Tommy, I found some blood on the jeans you left in the wash."

A pregnant pause ensued as he tried to think of an answer. Had she told the police? Might she have given them the jeans? "Aye, I cut my finger on some cutty grass. Why?" He hated lying to his mum.

"Just wondering, that's all."

"Nay big deal."

"How're Chrissie and the bairn?"

"Okay, sort of. Chrissie doesn't seem to want me back, but she's agreed to meet weekly so I can see wee Andy. Aye, I'm scared it's over for good and I don't know what to do."

"Oh, Tommy, don't think that way. They're your family now and you need to keep trying. She'll take you back—you're wee Andy's Da' and they need you. You'll see."

Ma always made things seem better.

After a pause, she continued. "What are you doing calling at this time anyway? Haven't you got a job yet?"

"Aye, I've got a job, as a cabbie. I've been working the graveyard shift."

"That's good news. Your Da' will be glad of that."

"I doubt it. I miss you Ma."

"Aye, and me. Take care Tommy and stay in touch, you hearing me?"

"Aye. Bye for now."

"Cherrio."

Guilt gnawed at his gut as he hung up the receiver. It was entirely his fault. He'd been stupid and he couldn't deny it. Could he ever make amends? Would he ever be free of it? The lass must have gone to the police. Were they still looking for him? They knew it was him—she'd known his name from the letter.

But now he was about to meet Chrissie.

Maybe Ma was right. Perhaps there is some hope.

*

Tommy scurried along the High Road in Finchley, aware he was late for his meeting with Chrissie. The street was busier than usual, probably something to do with the impending royal wedding. Demand for cabs had picked up and his shifts were getting stretched—twelve-hour nights were normal now. Tired and irritable, he'd need to make an effort to keep his temper in check. One more outburst and he could lose everything.

Inside the teashop, Chrissie sat holding his bairn at a table in the corner. The pram beside her was littered with rattles and baby accessories.

"Chrissie, sorry I'm late—it was work." He sat down next to her.

"Hi, Tommy. It doesn't matter. Andy's been content watching the goings-on."

"Can I hold him?" His troubles dissolved as they were replaced with another more powerful emotion that rose up and tightened his chest. He gave Andy a smile, and the bairn seemed to smile back.

"You take him while I get us a cuppa." Chrissie passed Andy to Tommy who held him delicately and tentatively, overcome by how small and helpless he was. A strong protective instinct made Tommy want to protect his wee bairn from all that was bad in the world.

"Andy, I'm your Da'."

Andy gurgled and grasped his fingers, as Chrissie returned with the tea.

"Chrissie, he's so bonnie."

Chrissie beamed and her dimple appeared for a moment. "He's a good boy, content most of the time. Hungry, though. He's taken to his solids really well."

They chatted some more, mostly superficial banter and nothing meaningful. Yet, in that moment, he felt his family was complete.

"Chrissie, you know I'm truly sorry for what I did to you. How can I make you see that?"

"I don't know. You lost your temper more than once and it was too easy for you to take it out on me. I've been learning about cycles of domestic abuse. It usually starts with tension that builds up to the abuse and ends with a honeymoon phase. And then it starts all over again, in ever decreasing circles. That was us, Tommy. That's the path we were on. I don't feel I can trust you not to start it all over again."

"Nay, that's no' us, Chrissie. You're overreacting. We're no' on that cycle. What's happened is behind us and I've said I'm sorry. Look, I promise I'll be a good husband and Da'. I know I will." His heart pounded loudly and his eyes welled up, taking him by surprise. Then the shame, he could almost hear his da' saying, 'Lads don't cry'. But he couldn't bear to lose her. "Chrissie, I want you to marry me—please. You'll see how good it'll be. I'm different, you must see that. I need you both."

"But that's just it. Would that be good for us, or just for you? You always make it about you. Can't you see that? You want me to marry you. Well what about me? What about Andy? I can't marry you, Tommy."

"Nay, Chrissie, please don't say that. I'm working now, and on the wages and tips, I can look after you—both o' you."

"Tommy, don't. Let's just let it be for now and we'll see how things work out. You know why I'm doing this. It's for Andy's sake as much as mine."

Deflated, he turned to Andy, while Chrissie drank her tea. There was nothing more to say.

How had they come to this? It'd been good at first, aye, they'd had fun. After he quit the Navy they'd found a bedsitter and moved in together. It'd upset her parents, but he hadn't cared. Those early days were one long date, and they were happy just spending time together. Work, money and family didn't seem to matter back then.

When had it started to go wrong? He'd always known he had a temper, that he'd occasionally lash out, but it didn't happen often. He couldn't recall what'd triggered it the first time things had gotten out of hand.

One time he'd been drinking with Dobbo and a few friends at the pub. That wasn't unusual—he'd always enjoyed a drink with the lads. This time, Chrissie had been visiting her parents and he was to join them for tea. But he'd forgotten the time—it was a mistake, that was all.

Then Chrissie had turned up at the pub with a real head of steam on. Eyes blazing, she'd given him a right dressing down in front of the boys. At first it was almost funny, but she'd kept on and on at him. They'd gone home and he'd hit her. Just once, with his fist. He hadn't meant to harm her. She'd looked startled at first, but then he'd seen the hurt in her eyes. She'd sported a black eye for days and he'd watched her trying to cover it with make-up, telling people she'd walked into a cupboard door. He'd tried to make it up to her, but she'd been aloof.

After that, things were never quite the same. They'd row over trivial matters. There were other times he'd hit her, not many, but slowly their relationship seemed to dismantle, until she'd announced she was leaving him. Gutted, he'd headed back to Lesmahagow. He found out about the bairn later, in a letter she sent.

The hurt was still raw. If only he could go back and do things differently. He shouldn't have lost his temper with her, but strewth, it hadn't been just his fault. She shouldn't have nagged him.

He and Chrissie had slipped further and further apart, with him continually messing up and nothing ever seemed to work out right. Now it seemed her fun-loving spirit had been replaced by a hard resolve—no doubt due to her parents' influence. Who knew what would make a difference now, but something had to change. He'd thought having a job would help, but it didn't seem to have made any impact. Maybe it was his fault—everything had always been his fault. That girl on the path hadn't asked for it. He was to blame there. Maybe Chrissie was right. Maybe they should lock him up and throw away the key.

"I have to go now, but I'll see you next week." Chrissie took Andy and settled him in the pram.

Downhearted, he watched her leave and headed back to the flat.

*

Tommy awoke from a fitful sleep to find Dobbo at home talking to his emaciated-looking flatmate, Jerome.

"Awrite, Dobbo?" Tommy asked. "Ach, thank goodness you're home—I've had a beggar of a time. Awrite, Jerome?"

"Hey, Tommy. Jerome and I were just talking about the flat—and we need to talk. You want a coffee?"

"Aye, coffee would be grand."

Jerome looked embarrassed. "Sorry, I can't stay. I was just on my way out. Catch you later." He pulled on his jacket before making a fast exit.

Tommy resented Jerome and was pleased he'd gone out. They had no common ground. Jerome, a trendy dresser, worked locally in an administrative job.

Dobbo made two mugs of coffee and they took them into the small living room, where they slumped onto the ragged couches surrounded by Tommy's discarded clothes and bedding.

Tommy eyed his friend closely. "What's up?"

"You know how I think of you like a brother and believe me, if it were up to me we wouldn't be needing to have this chat. But the flatmates have been complaining about you dossing on the couch. They want me to ask you to find a flat of your own." Dobbo squirmed on the sofa, avoiding eye contact.

"Ach, it's just a temporary measure until I sort things out with Chrissie. You know that."

"Yeah, I know, but they're not happy. I should've asked them before I offered it to you. It's not fair on them, and it's already been longer than we thought."

"Didn't think you'd hit a mate when he's down." Tommy stared at the floor, unable to look Dobbo in the eye.

"I'm sorry, but it's not my decision. Tommy, I have to listen to my flatmates. It's their place too."

"Aye. Is it Jerome's fault? He's always so grumpy."

"I admit he's been a bit off since coming back from his year backpacking around Asia. He'd a hard time of it over there. Have you noticed how sickly he looks?"

"Aye. Like starvation-on-stilts, and his face is pale and poxy."

"He came home from India, sick with dysentery. He's still not right." Dobbo stretched his legs out. "Don't take it personally."

Dejected, Tommy sipped his coffee. "When do they want me out?"

"I don't know, maybe a couple of weeks? You should be able to find a place by then. I'll keep my ear to the ground for you at the Jolly Miller. Bound to be someone there who knows of a flat." Dobbo sounded apologetic. "No hard feelings?"

"Aye, no hard feelings. I guess it's no' your fault." But Tommy couldn't ignore the niggling feeling of rejection. He'd had it with his dad when he was growing up, he'd had it at the hands of the bullies in the Navy, he'd had it with Chrissie. And now Dobbo was turning him out.

"If it were just up to me, I'd let you stay. You know that. How's it going with Chrissie?"

"Saw her today, but still no progress."

"Sorry to hear that."

"I had Andy in my lap. Aye, he's a bonnie bairn, that one."

"Blimey, I can't imagine being a dad. Chrissie will change her mind, you'll see."

"Nay, it's no' looking good. I thought if I could get a job..." His voice trailed off. "It's her parents' fault, I'm sure of it. They never did think I was good enough. Man, I'm sick of the toffs in this city. I have my share of them in the cab—think they're a cut above the rest of us."

"It's not so bad. There's lots of good folk 'bout these parts. The punters at the Jolly Miller are good salt-of-the-earth blokes. Just give it more time."

"Aye, maybe you're right. The long hours aren't helping. It's chaos out there just now and I won't be having any time off until after the royal wedding."

"How about a quick one before you start your shift? It's the least I can do for you." Dobbo chuckled. "Tell you what, let's head down to the Jolly."

9

Breakfast was nearly over when the phone rang at the Cohens. Rose could hardly contain her excitement. At this hour, it was likely to be someone from home.

"Rose, it's for you." Mrs Cohen held the receiver out to her and winked.

"Hello?"

"Rose, it's Gary."

Her pulse quickened and her cheeks were filled with warmth. "It's really good to hear your voice. Thanks *so* much for the roses, they're gorgeous. I couldn't believe it when the courier delivered them and said they were for me—that was a first. They are the most perfect red roses, three of them, wrapped beautifully."

"I'm glad you got them okay. I wasn't sure about Interflora from this distance. When I got your letter, I was so worried about you. Are you okay?"

His Kiwi accent sounded stronger than she remembered.

"I'm okay. I'm starting to get out and about more. It gave me a bit of a fright, but I just have to dig deep."

"Do you know if they've caught him?"

"No, I don't think so. I called the Lesmahagow police last week, but they all but dismissed me—as if they weren't the least bit interested." She paused, considering again the possible ramifications of not pressing charges, of him being out on the street ... "I hope I'm doing the right thing, you know, in not pressing charges."

"I'm sure you are. You need to put yourself first."

"But what if he does it again? It'd be on my conscience then, almost like an accomplice." It didn't bear thinking about.

"Don't even go there. He makes his choices, not you. You're the victim in all this."

"Well, I just hope I'm doing the right thing."

"Do you think you should come home? Or would it help if I come over?"

"No, I know you'd sacrifice your degree for me, but it's not necessary." She loved his concern. "I'd love you to be here and not just because of the mugging, but I'm okay. Mrs Cohen has been wonderfully supportive. I feel safe here and little Daniel is a welcome distraction. Besides, you need to finish your studies. Don't worry about me. I've just got to tough it out."

"Well, if you're sure. But I'm here for you."

"I know—thanks. I'm definitely planning to come home in November. I don't want to be away any longer—a year's long enough. I miss you."

"Me, too. I love you," he mumbled.

"I love you, too." She knew it was hard for him to say these words. He was a typical Kiwi bloke after all, and she loved him all the more for making the effort.

She talked a bit more about her travel plans and then Gary told her about life at university. He sounded happy enough, but it was clear he was missing her as much as she missed him. Not wanting it to end, but knowing the call would be costing him a small fortune, she reluctantly said goodbye. She replaced the receiver in the cradle, wanting to dance about the room. Instead, she hummed quietly as she cleared away the breakfast things.

*

She looked over her shoulder. A man rushed towards her, his hands reaching for her. She couldn't make out his face— it was as though he didn't have one. He wrestled her to the ground. His hands squeezed her throat. A kaleidoscope of revolving shapes came at her—orange, red, yellow, green, purple, then black, so black. Argh!

Rose bolted upright and tried to gather her thoughts. Her heart was racing and she was damp with sweat. She reached for the light switch, turned on the light, and looked at the small bedside clock. It was twenty past four in the morning. *Why does the dream keep coming back?*

Chocolate. She needed chocolate. She opened the drawer in the bedside table, took a Mars bar out from her secret stash, ripped it open and dropped the wrapper into the drawer. Almost ritualistically, she bit into it and sucked on it, savouring its sweetness, hoping for comfort. The sweet caramel chocolate oozed over her tongue and worked its magic.

I'm okay. I'm lucky to have had my ordeal and survived. I'm stronger and I know myself so much better. And I'm now safer too.

Chocolate and self-talk were habitual weapons that helped calm her down.

Afraid to turn out the light, she picked up her book to try and shake off the nightmare, but she was tired and distracted, making it difficult to read. She wanted sleep. Only two hours until she had to get up and prepare the family breakfast.

She turned out the light and rolled over and into a foetal position. Sleep came slowly.

*

A noise at the front door caught Rose's attention. She went through to the hall and collected the mail. A package was addressed to her. It was the photos from the film she'd sent away for developing and printing. Getting photos was always a highlight and she dropped the Cohen's mail into the study and raced up to her room.

At her desk, she tore open the package and took out the prints. One by one she looked at them. The first one was of Ted standing in front of his house in Lesmahagow. The boot shop was next, followed by the church and the excavations. She stopped. She knew what was coming. She breathed in deeply, releasing it slowly.

She turned over the print and froze. Lesmahagow from the old railway track—the old church with its tall spire dominated the scene and in the foreground was shrubbery with yellow flowering gorse. Her hand shook and her vision blurred as tears welled up and ran down her face. Her pulse raced and her skin became hyper-sensitive and sweaty. As if hot, she dropped the photos onto the desk and pushed them away.

She sobbed.

Finally, she pulled herself together and wiped her eyes. It was only a photo. She picked up the pile of discarded prints and flipped through them until she found the one. She looked at it again. *I survived. He's not going to get the better of me. I'm going to be okay.*

Calmer now, she looked at the other photos. But she'd lost her usual enthusiasm and needed a distraction. She busied herself with the dusting.

"Rose, phone for you," Mrs Cohen called from the study.

She went downstairs and, thanking her, took the receiver. "Hello, Rose speaking."

"Rose, it's Kathy. How're you doing?"

"Not too bad, thanks." She paused. "In fact I'm feeling loads better. I even swam in the pool yesterday when there was nobody about."

"That's great news. I've got a proposition for you. Why don't we go to the royal wedding?"

"We'd never get near it for the crowds. Wouldn't we be better watching it on the telly?"

"I reckon we should camp out on the street as close to St Paul's Cathedral as we can get. I'm going to ask Sharon for the time off. Want to join me?"

The familiar cramp tightened her stomach and goose bumps tingled along the back of her neck. *Could she?* "I don't know Kathy. It might be a bit soon for me."

"Rose, it'll be fine—you'll see. Stephanie says she's coming. There'll be crowds about and there's safety in numbers." Kathy's tone was reassuring.

"I guess I could talk to Mrs Cohen and see what she thinks."

"Great, it'll be fun. It's definitely a once-in-a-lifetime experience. You won't get that in Kiwi land."

Maybe Kathy was right. Rose had stayed on in London to be close to the action as the royal wedding hype unfolded. It'd be a shame if her fears prevented her from witnessing it firsthand. Anyone could see it on TV, but being there in the crowd would be amazing.

"Okay, you've convinced me. I'll see if I can get the time off. I'll call you back soon."

"That's great news. I know you won't regret it."

They talked some more about their plans for backpacking around Europe before Rose hung up and went to find Mrs Cohen.

*

The eve of the royal wedding between Prince Charles and Lady Diana Spencer had finally arrived, and Rose was taking the tube to Bank Station to meet Kathy and Stephanie. Feeling lucky to be in London at such an auspicious time, she was eager to secure a place in front of St Paul's Cathedral and to join in the revelry. The day was warm and she was dressed in jeans and a red short-sleeved open-neck shirt to reflect the festivities. She'd crammed her bag with a sweater and jacket for the night chill, suntan lotion, snacks, water, a rug and all the usual necessities—including her baton and pepper pot.

The atmosphere on the tube was different today. Strangers were acknowledging one another and smiling. There was lightness in the air, something she hadn't experienced since being in London. She'd never understood the fascination people had with the Royal Family. Why, even her mother would buy the New Zealand Woman's Weekly to read the latest gossip. Rose tended to be more in the republican camp, believing the Royals to be an unnecessary and extravagant burden on the taxpayer. But now, in London and witnessing first-hand the lead up to the royal wedding, she had become captivated by the fairy tale.

The middle-aged lady sitting next to her lowered her paper. "Going to the wedding?" the lady asked, her face beaming.

"Sure am. I imagine all of London will be there." Rose smiled back. "Are you?"

"No, I'm going to watch it on telly. I'm just going in to see the preparations. Where are you from?"

"New Zealand. It's going to be a real spectacle isn't it?"

"Yes. It's all anyone can talk about—the media's full of it. And we certainly need the distraction." The lady folded her paper up and placed it in her bag.

"I can't believe how big it is over here," Rose said. "But even at home they'll probably be staying up all night to watch it live."

"It's been a fairly dismal year otherwise for us Brits. We needed something to pick us up. The economy's been in recession and Thatcher's reforms have brought us high unemployment."

"Yes. And there were those terrible Brixton riots, and then the skinhead and punk riots. Once, I was out with a friend and we found ourselves right in the middle of a stand-off between angry skinheads and the police. It was really scary. We had to run down a side street to escape."

"Oh, that's awful. The violence and vandalism have been far more extreme and quite a worry this year. And to top it off, we've had the on-going problems with Northern Ireland and the bombings," the lady said. "You wonder where it will all end up. It's not the same Britain I grew up in."

Rose looked out the window as the train slowed and stopped at another station. She watched as a few passengers got out and more replaced them. The doors closed and they were off. "Are you a fan of the monarchy?"

"Many people have been saying the monarchy's archaic. But I think the royal engagement's fixed that. It's brought light into our depressed country and a renewed interest in the Royal Family—and we need them. Hopefully the tradition of the monarch will strengthen and live on long after we've gone."

"Lady Diana seems lovely, doesn't she?" Rose had been fascinated by the shy, unassuming future princess.

"Yes. Her picture is everywhere—she must be the most photographed woman around. I can't wait to see the wedding dress."

"Same here. I don't envy her being hounded by the press all the time."

"No. But a mere glance from her sells the papers. And she's influencing the fashions with her style."

"I love her style." Rose was of similar colouring, height and build to Lady Diana, piquing interest in her sense of fashion even more. Hairdressers advertised her hairstyle, dress shops carried copycat clothes, and shoe shops were flooded with her trademark low pump shoes. Lady Diana brought style to the Royal Family, and the wedding a ray of light in what was otherwise a bleak canvas.

If only the fairy tale magic could shine a light into her own darkness and banish fear from her kingdom.

The train pulled into the station and Rose, gathering up her things, exchanged goodbyes with the lady.

Rose left the train and almost skipped up the steps onto the street. Then she paused, captivated by a gaiety she hadn't experienced for some time. The sun was shining and everything looked clean, bright, and colourful. Even the buildings seemed to have taken on a cheerful appearance, their usually dowdy exteriors enhanced with planter boxes full of bright coloured flowers and Union Jacks waving in the breeze. A bus with a festive bow painted on its side went past. London was at its best and she soaked it all in, letting it wash over her and chase her tension away. Crowds milled about and there was an excited buzz of anticipation.

She checked her map to get her bearings. Ludgate Hill, where she was to meet the others, was to be part of the procession route as celebs and royalty made their way to St Paul's Cathedral the next day. It was only a short walk down Queen Victoria Street, which had already been closed off, onto St Paul's Churchyard and then to Ludgate Hill. The street was already teeming with people and her enthusiasm waned. Was this a good idea? What if she couldn't find the others?

Worried, she searched the crowd for Kathy's blonde curls. Before her angst could deepen into full-blown fear, she spotted her friend waving enthusiastically, Stephanie grinning beside her. Rose's unease vanished. They were standing on the kerbside in a prime spot right opposite St Paul's. She wove her way through the crowds and greeted them with a hug.

"Hey Kathy, Steph—it's good to see you both."

"Hi Rose. We've marked the spot." Kathy grinned.

"Rose, welcome to our little party."

"Wow, you're both looking festive." Rose took in Kathy's red and white striped top and Stephanie's yellow hat, which was stunning against her dark hair.

"We need to stand out on the telly." Kathy laughed. "Have you heard they're expecting six hundred thousand people to line the streets tomorrow, and they're saying the wedding will be broadcast to seven hundred and fifty million viewers? And we'll be in the front row."

"Well, in one of the front rows, but maybe not *the* front row. We can't upstage the Queen." Pondering this, she added, "I wonder if our friends and families back home will see us?"

"Maybe. It's such a privilege to be here, don't you think?"

"Yep, a once-in-a-lifetime experience, that's for sure," Rose said. "I'm glad you talked me into coming. I'd have been gutted if I hadn't made the effort."

They chatted as they settled in to wait the twenty-four hours until the bride would arrive and reveal her much-anticipated dress to the world.

The street turned into one great party and strangers were unified in their common quest to watch the pomp and ceremony. London bobbies and armed forces personnel mingled with the crowd, exchanging friendly banter. Gone was the riot gear and tear gas seen in recent months. Speakers overhead broadcast announcements and relayed music.

Rose took turns with Kathy and Stephanie to guard their spot and their gear so they could each take a break and purchase food and drinks. Day turned into night and the party intensified as the street filled with revellers. She chatted with strangers and danced and sang throughout the night. It was the largest street party she'd ever seen.

A man danced his way towards her, linking arms with first one woman then another, spinning each around before repeating his dance with yet another. On and on he went, as he advanced towards her. Fascinated, she allowed him to link his arm through hers and she blushed as he spun her about breathlessly. And then he was gone, continuing his routine towards the steps of St Paul's.

Another man grabbed her hand and pulled her to her feet and they danced to the songs of Freddie Mercury. It was madness and yet it was wonderful. Entertained, they barely noticed the hours passing.

Gone was the anxiety that had plagued her. Instead, there was safety in the crowd and she was able to relax and be truly happy. She even managed to curl up in her rug on the kerb and doze for an hour or two sometime before daybreak.

Dawn heralded the coming of the twenty-ninth of July. Barriers were placed in front of the kerbs and the street was swept one last time. Vans delivered flowerpots to line the procession route with colour. Police trotted their horses up and down the street. Amused, Rose watched a street cleaner pick up some horse manure with a silver brush and pan. Perhaps it was exhaustion, but everything appeared surreal.

Rose, along with Kathy and Stephanie, held onto their place at the front, with a clear view of the steps leading up to St Paul's Cathedral. The crowd of bystanders flooded in and pressed them against the barrier, but they stood their ground. Thankfully, uniformed policemen stood every six feet or so along the road, intent on keeping the crowd orderly and helping her to feel secure. Rose posed for a photo beside a young bobby with St Paul's as the backdrop. The buzz in the crowd rose as the time drew nearer. Up above, office windows were stacked full of onlookers.

"I hear some of them paid over one hundred and fifty pounds for a window place," Stephanie said. "That's six weeks' pay for us."

"I'd rather be down here, on the cheap and amongst the pageantry," Rose said.

"For sure, even if I had the money."

Hearing the crowd clap and cheer up the street from them, she turned to see a black sedan making its way towards them at walking pace. The crowd reacted like a Mexican wave, following its progress towards St Paul's. She didn't know who they were, but it didn't matter. The procession was beginning.

She clapped and cheered with the crowd as the cars slowly came along the prescribed route to St Paul's. She'd read that 2500 guests were expected to fill the great cathedral. British and foreign royalty. Past and present prime ministers, presidents, emperors and a variety of politicians. Celebrities—authors, artists, film stars, singers and musicians. And aristocrats and playboys, clergy, military representatives, stylists and members of the royal household. The crowd roared with laughter when Spike Milligan got out of his car and worked the crowd with his antics as he ventured towards St Paul's.

With a royal wave, the Queen and Prince Philip passed in a horse-drawn open coach and pulled up at the steps of St Paul's Cathedral. Rose cheered them on with the crowd.

And then it was the groom's turn. Prince Charles, escorted by Prince Andrew, arrived in a red open coach pulled by four white horses. He looked almost handsome in the uniform of a navy commander.

The crowd shifted about in anticipation. A loud cheer in the distance moved slowly closer, signalling something big was about to happen. Flanked by guards, a blue and gold glass coach drew near, sparkling in the sunlight and resembling something out of a fairy tale.

Inside sat the Lady Diana with her father. The soon-to-be-princess waved and smiled shyly as she passed. She looked stunning in her wedding dress. An enthusiastic roar went up from the crowd and Rose cheered with them. The roar became a collective gasp as the bride was helped out of the coach, her ivory taffeta dress shimmering in the sunlight. She seemed to glide up the steps as her attendants laid out her ridiculously long train behind her. The crowd went wild.

Rose listened to the service broadcast over loudspeakers. When the nervous bride tripped over her prince's names, Rose cheered her on with the crowd as if absolving her of any embarrassment. It added richness to the fairy tale about the commoner who married a prince.

The clear voice of Kiri Te Kanawa singing *Let the bright Seraphim* brought pangs of homesickness mixed with national pride. A lump formed in Rose's throat and tears welled.

And then it was nearly over, and the heat began to get the better of her. She felt light-headed, standing there with the crowd hemming her in, hot and sleep-deprived. She sat down behind the barrier with Kathy and Stephanie, which was no small feat given the pressure from the crowd behind.

Finally, the bride and groom and their guests emerged from the great building and walked down the steps to their waiting carriages. Rose watched the Royal Family depart for Buckingham Palace, before making her escape with Kathy and Steph in tow until it was time for them to go their own separate ways home. Rose paused, reluctant to make her journey alone. But buoyed by her experience, she hugged them before setting off for Bank Station. Even having to push through the crowds couldn't ruin her mood. She had witnessed a true fairy tale and a piece of British history in the making. She found her platform and boarded the train home, content.

As with the British public, the royal wedding had shone a light into her life, dimming the hurtful memories and dulling her fears. The day marked a milestone and she was filled with hope for her future, determined to overcome her fears and put the ordeal behind her. She'd stayed working in

London to see this event and now she was about to begin her travels. She welcomed the challenge of discovering foreign places with a mixture of anticipation and apprehension, unsure what her backpacking adventures would bring.

Life was starting to feel good again.

10

London was buzzing on the eve of the royal wedding and Tommy was frustrated. The city streets had all but come to a standstill with the traffic. Shops were selling all manner of paraphernalia to celebrate the day and turn a quick profit—mugs and plates, buttons and flags, pens and postcards, scarves and tee shirts. It was madness and Tommy's minicab hadn't stopped all week.

He pulled up outside the address in Golders Green and tooted the horn. Two attractive young women in sunglasses came out of the house and sauntered towards the waiting minicab carrying overnight bags. The flip-flops on their feet signalled that they were from the Antipodes and he guessed they were nannies or housekeepers to wealthy Jewish families.

The short one with blonde curly hair opened the rear door of the cab and said, "Ludgate Hill, please." He was suddenly anxious as he perceived a New Zealand accent.

"Aye, but we have a problem. That area is already closed off for the royal wedding."

"No worries, mate. Just take us as close as you can to St Paul's. We want to get a good spot for the wedding tomorrow," the tall slim one said, as she pushed her long black wavy hair behind her ear.

"Aye, I'll do my best. But the traffic round there is heavy and we might get caught up."

The girls piled into the back seat.

He listened to their chatter as he navigated the busy streets. The accent disturbed him and he was a little panicked—his instinct was to run, but he knew that was ridiculous. It didn't take much to transport him back to the old railway track and to his meeting with the New Zealand girl. His guilt was making him paranoid and he knew it. If only he could make amends. It was hard to recognise the monster he'd become—it disgusted him to think he was some sort of perverted deviant. It was little wonder Chrissie didn't want him.

"Excuse me, I was asking how long it would take to get into the city?"

"Sorry. It's hard to say because of the traffic. Maybe an hour or thereabouts?"

"Crikey, that's longer than we thought. We're meant to be meeting friends there."

"Are you both from New Zealand?"

"No way. We're Aussies," the blonde one replied. "Kiwi's talk funny. If you wanna tell the difference, ask them to say 'fish and chips'!"

"Fush en chups," the dark one said and they both went into hysterics.

Tommy relaxed. "You here on a working holiday?"

"Sure are. We're both working for families in Golders Green. You sound Scottish—how long have you been driving cabs round London?"

"Ach, no' long."

"Like it?"

"Aye, it's okay. It's a job, but the wedding has us busy this week. The shifts are long, but there's some good tips to make up for it."

"Don't count on it," one of them sniggered.

"Aye." Antipodeans were famous for their poor tipping.

The girls were friendly enough, chatting amicably as he drove through the mayhem around St Paul's, dropping them off three blocks from their destination. His spirits had lifted, and he found his next fare with ease.

His passengers on this shift were mainly party goers out patronizing the bars and clubs lubricating the great street party that preceded the royal wedding. He'd learned the trick of parking up and standing outside a bar.

"Minicab!" he'd shout, and his persistence would be rewarded, despite the presence of several minicab drivers all competing for fares. He could barely hide his resentment for the predominantly white-collar workers with upper-class attitudes, who invariably treated him with disdain. And yet, when they were legless—as so often they were in the wee hours—they were no better than he and his friends who'd left school early to drum up work if and where they could. They made him feel inadequate and he could almost hear his father's echo in their unspoken words.

As dusk turned into the wee hours, he grew more and more disenchanted.

Finally his long and gruelling shift ended and he headed home to the flat. Finding the flatmates yet to rise, he made toast and tea, turned on the television and settled down to watch a replay of the footy game between Celtic and Rangers. Fully absorbed in the game, he was disturbed by a loud knocking at the door, which he reluctantly left the telly to open.

A stern-faced policeman in uniform stood before him. Fear unleashed a rush of adrenalin and his pulse raced. He stared at the policeman, too scared to speak.

"Is there a Tommy Stewart here?" The uniformed stranger gave him a dark look.

A door opened behind him. "Who is it, Tommy?" He turned to see Jerome standing in the hall in his pyjamas.

He had no choice. "Aye, that'd be me." His heart pounded as he tried to look calm.

"Sergeant Jones, Metropolitan Police. Can I have a word? It won't take long."

"Aye, what's up?" The time of reckoning had come.

"Are you Tommy Stewart of Lesmahagow?"

"Aye."

"We've received a complaint about an alleged incident that took place in Lesmahagow last month. Can you tell me where you were on the eleventh of June?"

"I think I was back here then—or perhaps I was still in transit." Desperate, he tried to sound vague and hoped Jerome wouldn't remember the date he'd arrived. "Why?"

"A woman was attacked in Lesmahagow. We're just making routine inquiries." The bobby seemed to study him. "Are you sure you weren't in Lesmahagow on that date?"

Not wanting to react, Tommy tried to look calm. "Like I said, I can't remember exactly what date I came south. Sorry I can't help more. I hope the tourist is okay." His gut spasmed at his mistake—he'd just called her a *tourist*. But the words were out and he could only hope his slip would go unnoticed.

"Nothing too serious. Do you know a New Zealand woman by the name of Rose Wells?"

His throat constricted as his panic escalated. "Nay, sorry. Can't say I've met a New Zealander before." *How much did they know?* "Look, if you don't mind, I've just come off a long shift and I need a kip."

"We have reason to believe that you were in Lesmahagow on the date in question and you were named by the victim. As yet, she's not ready to press charges."

Tommy maintained a poker face.

"Nice shirt. You a Celtic fan then?"

Caught off guard, Tommy grinned, "Aye, sure am. Do you follow them then?"

"Me, I'm a Spurs supporter. Where did you get your shirt?"

"I got it from a mate. Why?"

"It looks a lot like the shirts taken in a ram raid last week." He looked hard at Tommy.

Unable to hold his gaze, Tommy looked down at the floor. He could feel himself shaking and was terrified the bobby would see it too.

"Know this Tommy Stewart, we *will* be watching you." The bobby scribbled in his notebook before pulling a card out of his pocket and handing it to Tommy. "If you have anything you want to tell me, call me on this number."

Heat flushed his cheeks as he reached out to take the card with a clammy hand. The bobby turned and walked back down the steps.

"What was all that about?"

Tommy had forgotten Jerome standing behind him. He shut the door and turned to look at him. "Ach, it must be a mistake."

"Interesting." Jerome sounded less than convinced.

"I've had a long shift. I'm off ta bed." Tommy walked back to the sitting room, closing the door behind him.

Now what?

He was wide awake with the adrenalin surging through his body and he could feel the sweat. *This is it then. The consequences are finally catching up with me.* Panicked by the thought the tide had turned in this whole ugly affair, he paced the room. *Should I run? But if I do, where should I go?* A sudden taste of acid and he dashed to the bathroom, where he lurched over the toilet bowl. Head down, he allowed the fluid to flow as if he were purging out the guilt. Once spent, he washed his face and rinsed his mouth before returning to the sitting room, closing the door behind him.

"Tommy?" It was Dobbo.

"Aye, come in."

Dobbo was wearing pyjama pants and an old and faded Levi tee shirt. He looked like he'd just woken up. "What's up?" He rubbed his eyes.

"Nay, don't ask. You don't want to know."

"It's a hell of a time to be making a racket. I'm knackered— didn't finish at the Jolly until after midnight." Dobbo eyed his friend more closely before asking, "You in trouble?"

"Aye, but it's complicated. I hurt someone, back in Lesmahagow."

"Bloody hell! What happened?"

"I beat up this lass—cripes, it was nearly two months ago and I thought I'd got away with it. But now it looks like she went to the cops after all." Angry with himself, he picked up one of the discarded shirts lying on the couch and slung it across the room. "Help me, Dobbo. Strewth. I don't want to go to the slammer for this."

"How bad was it?"

"The bobby said she was okay."

"Are they going to charge you?"

"Who knows? It doesn't seem like she's pressed charges—at least not yet."

"Then they can't do anything."

"But if she's gone to the cops, why wouldn't she press charges? Do you think she still could?"

"Hard to say, but I'd have thought it unlikely now. Who was she?"

"I dunno—some tourist."

"Then she's probably not even in the UK. You'll be okay. If she hasn't pressed charges already, then odds are she won't now."

Did he dare hope for this? "I feel sick. Dobbo, I don't know what drove me to do it—I just lost it. I wish I could turn back the clock. Gawd, what should I do?"

Dobbo stifled a yawn. "Don't get your trews in a twist! Like I said, if he didn't take you in, you have to assume they haven't got what they need to arrest you. It's a bleedin' mess, but I'm guessing you'll be okay. Best get some kip." He slapped Tommy on the shoulder and left the room, closing the door behind him.

Tommy could hear the chatter coming from the other flatmates in the kitchen. He knew they were talking about him, but right now he was too upset to face them. He lit a fag and paced up and down as he wrestled with his thoughts.

*

Later that day and badly lacking in sleep, Tommy walked into the smoky cab office down the back street in Golders Green, ready for another shift. Dave the controller was at his desk and deep in conversation with John, Tommy's cab owner. A group of older cabbies jabbered over a game of cards, the type decorated with topless ladies. Their dirty formica table was littered with coffee mugs, overflowing ash trays, and packets of smokes and matches. They were the 'in crowd', Dave's mates and favourites.

One of the card players looked at Tommy and called, "Oi, porridge wog!" The others laughed, reminding him of those dark Navy days.

"'Ere, take no notice of the smarmy tosser." John signalled him to come over.

Tommy gave a two-finger salute to the card players, anxiety giving way to anger.

Dave eyeballed him. "Jock, you alright?"

The nickname irritated him but he answered. "Aye, what's up?"

"I got some new stuff. You interested?"

Tommy looked across at the piles of footy shirts on the shelves that lined the back wall of the base. Just last week, he'd bought the Celtic shirt for ten quid, a real bargain. The base served as a fence for stolen goods, and he'd seen some shady characters unload vanloads of all manner of stuff.

Word had it that they were the product of ram raids. Vans would reverse into a shop front to break the glass, then they'd grab as much as they could before the cops showed up. The formula seemed to be working as ram raids were common round these parts, enabling thieves to support their drug habits. Minicab bases were a good fence, with the controller buying the goods and then on-selling to the cabbies, while taking a cut.

"Nay. Best not." The bobby's visit had scared Tommy.

"Come on. Don't be a wuss. It's a bargain."

"What you got?" He couldn't resist looking.

"Fancy some gold? Or a watch? Real good quality it is. Take a look."

Dave pulled a tray out from a drawer. It was loaded with shiny gold chains of all types and sizes. But then Tommy remembered the look on that bobby's face when he'd seen his Celtic shirt. No. Best not even look at the merchandise.

Dave, still gawping at him, said, "A nice touch for the girlfriend."

Chrissie had always liked jewellery. Maybe if he took her a nice chain she might relent and agree to move in with him. It would prove he was doing well. He picked up a heavy gold chain that'd look good on him. Imagine Ma's face when she saw him coming with this around his neck. She'd be so proud he'd made it. He picked up another shorter piece.

"Lady's bracelet—good heavy quality, and cheap," Dave said. "Twenty-five quid and it's yours. You won't get a bargain like that anywhere else."

Tommy curled it around his own wrist. Tempting.

They were interrupted by the phone. Dave answered it and scribbled an address down before hanging up. Instead of picking up the RT, he called out to the card players, "Who's for an airport job?"

"I'll take it." One of the older guys got to his feet and took the paper from Dave.

Aggravated by the interchange, Tommy returned his attention to the gold. Pointing to the first chain, he asked, "How much?"

"A good geezer's chain that one, and it'll be sure to impress the ladies. Feel the weight. Can sell that to you for just forty—it's another bargain at that. You can sure pick 'em, Jock."

Tommy hesitated. Sixty-five quid and he still owed John forty, but with all the hours he'd been working, he nearly had enough for both.

"Some of the cabbies have turned a tidy profit selling them on," Dave continued.

He could imagine the look on Chrissie's face when he gave it to her. Aye, he'd have to do it. And it wouldn't hurt to wear a gold chain himself—it would impress her parents. He turned to John, pulling out some notes from his jeans pocket. "Here's the forty quid I still owe you." He counted what was left and found he had only fifty-five. Looking now at Dave, he asked, "Can I take those two chains and owe you a tenner?"

"Cripes, what do you think this is—a charity?" He reached out and quickly took the notes from Tommy. "A tenner tonight, okay?" he said as he handed the chains over.

Slipping them into his pocket, Tommy replied, "Aye, I'll be good for it."

*

The shift passed slowly with Tommy preoccupied over the bobby's visit. Normally he'd find the variety of the people he picked up interesting enough. However tonight he avoided their small talk as a cloud of impending doom made him jittery. Even the gold chain around his neck didn't cheer him up.

In the wee hours towards the end of his shift, he was in Hampstead Heath having just delivered a punter to a flat. The radio had been quiet and there were no black cabs about, so he decided to pull into a cab rank near what he'd heard was a popular back street club. Loud music was playing close by and he figured it shouldn't be long before someone came out looking for a ride home. Exhausted, he stretched himself out in his seat and yawned so much his eyes watered. A sharp tap on his window shocked him awake and dread filled his senses. Instead of the cop he expected, he could just make out a bloated face under a black cap.

"Get your useless pile of junk off my rank!" The irate cabbie pulled open the door.

"Nay, hold up..."

"I'm sick of you lowlifes not sticking to the rules." The cabbie took a swing at him, landing a blow across his face.

Tommy felt a crack and pain erupted in his cheekbone and through his nose. For a moment everything seemed to go black and then he was being pulled from the minicab.

"They should hang the lot of you for poaching."

Tommy hit the ground before he could gather his senses. He scrambled to his feet and flung himself at the man, wrestling him to the ground. They writhed about as he fought to get the better of the cabbie. His rival had the larger frame and was heavy, but Tommy was muscular and agile. Tommy pulled a knee hard up into the man's groin, and he doubled up in pain.

Tommy freed his right arm and landed a powerful punch into the cabbie's unprotected face. His head jerked sharply backwards forcing him to release his grip on Tommy who scrambled to his feet. He picked the man's cap up from where it'd fallen and put it on his own head before getting into his cab. Soon the cops would be swarming the place, so he cranked the ignition and sped off down the road towards the base. His head hurt and he could feel his face swelling.

Stuff their stupid rules. Serves him bloody well right!

11

Rose stood in the middle of London's Victoria Station, her backpack slung over her shoulders, almost overwhelmed by the press of people around her. They scurried along, intent on their purpose, oblivious to her dilemma. Should she take the train to Stonehenge for a day excursion and wait in England for Kathy before heading across the Channel, or head for Carmen in Germany alone? Kathy had another week of work before she could start their backpacking adventures and Rose was eager to start.

The sheer enormity of the station was intimidating with its high roof held by massive curved steel girders, leaving her feeling small and insignificant. Large archways separated the expansive areas, dotted with small kiosks selling a myriad of foods, drinks and curiosities. Above her were boards with multitudinous columns of information announcing platforms for arrivals and departures. Scanning it, she found the train to Dover would soon be leaving from Platform Twelve. *Should I go?* If she took the Dover train, she would barely have time to sort her ticket, let alone get money out and call Kathy.

Come on girl, where's your sense of adventure? Without further thought, she strode over to the ticket office and then raced across to the row of public phone booths alongside the Bureau de Change. Dropping some coins into one, she dialled Kathy's number. Kathy sounded surprised when Rose hurriedly outlined her change of plan but agreed to meet at Carmen's place in a week. A quick check of the station clock and she made a mad dash to the waiting train, zigzagging her way through the crowds.

The trip passed with ease. The train pulled into Dover in time for her to catch the eleven-forty sailing to Oostende. It was an easy connection from Oostende to Brussels, using her Eurorail pass for the first time. Sitting in the train, she listened to the foreign tongues and the enormity of what she was doing hit her. It was her first time in a non-English speaking country and she was on her own. The rest of the journey was spent worrying whether she'd made the right decision, but it was too late to turn back. She'd need to be vigilant, cautious and not too trusting. Her day pack contained her survival kit, the gift from Bill. She slipped her hand into the pack, fingering the baton and pepper pot.

The train pulled into Brussels on time at seven in the evening, and it was already getting dark outside, making her even more nervous. Seeing a Bureau de Change kiosk near the exit, she hurried over to change some traveller's cheques. Now she needed a youth hostel.

Looking for an information desk, she found instead a large map of the city taking centre place in the hall. She stood studying it, but it wasn't in English meaning she couldn't find where she was, let alone where she was going.

A man walked towards her.

"Excuse me, do you speak English?" she asked. "Um— parlez vous Anglais?"

"Non." He hurried away.

An older woman came along with a younger woman who looked like her daughter. She stepped in front of them and again asked, "Parlez vous Anglais?"

"Oui, a little," the older woman said, smiling at Rose.

Rose spoke slowly, hoping they would understand her. "Please, can you help me? I'm looking for the youth hostel."

The lady frowned and conversed rapidly with her daughter in a language Rose couldn't understand.

"Um, the youth hostel, YHA?" Rose tried again, hoping to make them understand.

"Yes, yes. It is here." The younger woman pointed to the map. "But it is not safe, not for a woman alone. It is, how do you say it? It is the red-light district."

Rose's stomach clenched and a chill spread down her spine. The old terror.

The woman was conversing some more with her daughter.

Feeling panicked, Rose looked at the map again. Pointing to a spot, she asked, "Excuse me, is this where we are?"

"Oui. But, please, you come home with us. We have, how do you say?" She looked at her daughter.

Her daughter finished her sentence. "We have spare room. Please, come."

"Thank you, but I couldn't." Although they appeared to be good folks, she was unsure of trusting strangers, especially when English wasn't their first language.

"Please, we insist. You see my older daughter, she is backpacking in Asia and the people are so kind. We would like to repay their kindness by helping you." The warmth radiated from the older woman's smile.

They looked harmless enough, and the last thing Rose wanted was to traipse off to the red-light district in the dark in search of a youth hostel. It really wasn't much of a choice and so she returned their smile. "Thanks, but are you sure? I really appreciate your offer."

"Yes, of course." The woman extended her hand to Rose and they shook. "I am Fleur Janssens and this is my daughter Hilda."

"And I'm Rose."

"Come!" Fleur gestured towards the exit and they left the station together.

The drive from the station was short and they were soon inside a small, but tidy apartment somewhere in Brussels. Mattheus, Fleur's husband, was home reading the paper and Fleur introduced them, explaining he couldn't speak English. Without a common language, they could only nod and smile at each other. She was shown to her room. It was small, with a single bed under a window hidden behind pretty floral curtains. The pink spread was home to several old stuffed toys including a tatty teddy bear and a rag doll that was missing one eye. A wooden bureau stood near the door and next to it was a pinboard with pictures of a tanned young woman who looked like Hilda, standing in front of some Asian landmarks and smiling.

Back in the living room, Fleur was preparing the evening meal. Rose chatted to Hilda as together they set the table.

"Your English is very good," Rose said.

"Thank you. Our native language is Flemish, which is similar to Dutch," Hilda said. "In Belgium, we speak many languages fluently. Belgium has many neighbours and so we have Dutch, French and German native speakers. I study languages at university in Antwerpen and am fluent in five."

Genuinely impressed, Rose said, "Wow, I can only speak English, and then not always very well."

"We have to speak these languages because they are spoken in the shops."

The atmosphere was congenial, but even so Rose felt tense and remained on guard. It was a struggle to put on the appearance of looking relaxed so as not to offend her hosts. But as the night passed without incident, her confidence grew and she enjoyed their company. It didn't take too long before she and Hilda were chatting away like old friends, comparing university experiences and life in their respective countries. If this was indicative of how her backpacking would go, roll on the rest of the adventure.

*

The horrifying images taunted her as she woke up in the unfamiliar bed, her heart pounding and her body bathed in sweat. It was the same old nightmare—always the same. He was faceless, and yet she'd seen his eyes. They were speckled brown with tiny pupils and they bored into her, drilled through her. *Why does he still have this power over me?*

Fully alert now, she absorbed her strange surroundings as her eyes adjusted to the gloom. She hoped she hadn't cried out and woken her hosts. She couldn't help but wonder who her assailant was—her memory had blanked out his name—and what had become of him. Still disturbed by the nightmare, she curled into a foetal position and hugged herself to try and calm her nerves. Sleep came fitfully.

*

Rose awoke in the strange bed, the nightmare still lingering. She could hear cheerful chatter coming from the dining room and she dressed in order to join her hosts.

"Morning." She forced a bright smile, not wanting to appear rude.

"Morning." Hilda beamed back at her. "Rose, I have no school today and you must stay another day and tour the city with me on bicycles. It is such a nice day, and I can show you the tourist sites. You can ride my sister's bicycle."

"I was planning to go on to my friend's place in Germany."

"What is the rush? We could have so much fun."

Carmen wasn't expecting her to arrive today. And there wasn't a single reason why she shouldn't stay another day and explore the city with her new friend. "I'd love to— Germany can wait until tomorrow." The spontaneity of her decision felt good and her mood began to lift.

"Rose, I am so excited to be your tourist guide. And I can practice more English on you."

Wearing bike-friendly clothes, she followed Hilda downstairs to the laundry where two bikes leaned against the wall. They were vintage type with a single gear, a basket over the front wheel and an old-fashioned bell on the handlebars. A 1950's floral dress and bonnet would have been the perfect accessory.

They wheeled the bikes outside, chatting, and Rose fell in behind her guide, bumping along the cobbled streets.

Hilda cheerfully pointed out various landmarks along their route. It was hard not to be affected by the beautifully warm and sunny day.

First stop was a sixty-one-centimetre-tall bronze statue of a little boy urinating into a fountain.

"This dates back to 1619," Hilda said. "We are very proud of this boy. It is called *Manneken Pis*, which means 'Little boy pee'."

"What does he stand for?"

"There are many legends, but according to Flemish folklore he became a hero when he put out a fire by urinating on it."

"He must have had a very full bladder." Rose chuckled.

Hilda responded with a loud laugh, enticing Rose to join in.

Despite everything, the nightmare continued to cast a shadow and Rose began to share her story to lessen its load. This time however, she was more detached than at other times, almost as if it was someone else's story. Hilda looked shocked as she listened, making sympathetic noises and encouraging Rose.

"It's strange but I can't remember my attacker's name any more, and yet I knew it," Rose said. "And I find myself thinking about him a lot, wondering if he got help and whether he sorted his problems out."

"Poor you. It was a horrible experience." Hilda's expression was full of concern. "Not remembering his name is a sign that you are getting better. I think sometimes God does these things to heal us and protect us from our fears."

"I hope so, but why let me have nightmares?"

"They will fade away. You will see."

"Thank you for listening." Rose smiled at Hilda. "You know, it helps me to share my story. The more I do, the more I seem to be able to distance myself from its reality."

Hilda's face lit up. "Perhaps it is like the story of *Manneken Pis*. The flames are your fears and like the boy, you need to put an end to them before they grow too big and consume you. Fears can grow out of proportion if you let them. But I think you are doing a good job—travelling alone is proof of that. You will overcome. I know this already."

"Are you saying I need to urinate on my fears?" Rose asked with a chuckle. Hilda hugged her as she dissolved into rapturous laughter.

All of the residual tension from the night had vanished and Scotland suddenly seemed a long way away, as were her fears. The challenge of travelling alone and being immersed in a foreign country was not so difficult and her confidence was building. Her theory, that having endured her bad luck the odds would be in her favour, was proving to be a good one.

Rose took out her camera and they giggled some more as Hilda posed for the photo in front of *Manneken Pis*.

"Come, let me show you some more of my home." Hilda picked up her bike and was off, with Rose in pursuit. They continued to cycle about the city, enjoying the sights and each other's company. They wound up at a local pub, sampling Belgian beer with mussels and fries—the perfect end to the perfect day. Life was good indeed.

*

The next day after breakfast, Rose reluctantly said goodbye to Fleur and Mattheus, hugging them close. She was grateful for the revival of her spirit, which she attributed to this hospitable family.

Hilda had volunteered to take Rose to the station and they grazed their way through the morning as Hilda wanted her to sample everything Flemish. They'd fast become good friends and it was easy to spend the time together. The morning disappeared and Rose found herself loading her things into Hilda's small car.

Back at the train station, Hilda helped her to make sense of the schedule and platforms. Carmen lived on the outskirts of the small German town of Berne. Rose's plan was to take the train to Bremen, changing at Köln. By her calculations, Bremen was only forty kilometres from Carmen's and so she'd call once there, hoping Carmen could come and pick her up. The next train to Köln was leaving in just fifteen minutes and it was yet another mad scramble. She hated saying goodbye to Hilda, wishing for more time with her new friend.

With her backpack on her back and her day pack clasped firmly in front, she rushed through the gate and headed for the platform.

12

London

Tommy woke up to his alarm and winced as he moved his head on the pillow, recalling the events of the previous night. His cheek and nose throbbed, and the knuckles on his right hand were red and puffy. He lifted his head off the blood-stained pillow, and sat up slowly, carefully, gingerly.

John would be angry when he heard. It was his cab and the black cab driver had probably taken down the registration. Would he call the police? Tommy couldn't afford to get into any more scrapes with the law—and they wouldn't need much of an excuse to nab him.

What was I thinking?

It'd been seven weeks since he'd started driving the cab, and he knew the city cab ranks were exclusively for the black cabs. But you'd think at that hour if you were quick, you could get away with a brief stop. Anyway, if the controller played fair, he wouldn't need to use the ranks to pick up fares.

It wasn't all bad though. Tommy was meeting Chrissie and wee Andy this afternoon. He reached out for his jacket and felt in the pocket for the chain bracelet. He couldn't wait to see Chrissie's face when he gave it to her. His tiredness evaporated just thinking about it, and he got off the couch and headed for the bathroom.

The flat was quiet and he assumed the others would be at work. Even so, he shut the door to the bathroom before going over to the vanity. The reflection in the mirror shocked him and he stood mesmerised, his eyes roving from the bright gold chain at the base of his neck to the lop-sided face streaked with dried blood. His right cheek was flushed and swollen under a puffy eye showing signs of turning black. But his worst feature was his fat and crooked nose, which looked like it might be broken.

He filled the cracked and grimy sink with cold water and splashed it over his face until the blood disappeared and his head had cleared. The red-tinged water reminded him of washing away the evidence that terrible afternoon he wished he could forget.

Downcast, he took the towel and dabbed his face dry, trying not to cause too much pain. Back to the sitting room, he changed into his Celtic shirt and jeans, and slipped the bracelet into his pocket. After a quick snack and a few painkillers washed down with a swill of water from the tap, he hurried out of the flat.

Worrying thoughts of the day before unsettled him. Not only did he feel threatened the copper might come looking for him, but if the girl pressed charges, what would they do him for? He wouldn't cope in the slammer—it'd be the end of him. And now he had the added worry of the fight last night. Although it didn't seem fair, he knew he was the one who'd broken the law. To top it off, he hadn't even begun to look for another flat. It'd been a few weeks since Dobbo had raised it and he was in danger of outstaying his welcome. He kept hoping Chrissie would change her mind—maybe today she'd agree they could find a flat together.

His head pounded as he rushed to catch the tube that would take him to the familiar meeting place. Anticipating how grateful she'd be over the bracelet took the edge off his stress levels. He exited the tube and navigated the station until he was once again on the High Road. It was a cooler day, and the street was quieter than usual. The pounding in his head had settled into a dull ache.

Chrissie was already seated in the tea shop and he was delighted that wee Andy was with her, happily sitting on her knee.

"Awrite?" He kissed her on the cheek and received the gentle flicker of her lips on his skin.

She pulled back and looked aghast as she studied his wounds. "What's happened to you? Have you been in a fight, Tommy Stewart?"

"Just took a hit from a bad-tempered cabbie." A suspicious look clouded her face and he added, "No big deal." He tried to smile but his face hurt too much.

"So—you still like to talk with your fists instead of your words?"

Her words cut deep.

"It wasn't like that, honest." He took a packet of fags out of his pocket and pulled one out. "Give me a chance. This was in self-defence, honest to God. I promise."

"Do you have to smoke over Andy?" Chrissie's eyes flashed with annoyance.

Ignoring her, but wanting to avoid a row, he put the fags away and reached out to take Andy.

Andy snuggled into his lap making happy noises, and Tommy kissed him gently on the neck. Andy giggled and snuggled even more. Tommy remembered the present and reached into his pocket and fingered it. "Chrissie, I have something for you. Shut your eyes and put out your hand."

"Tommy, I don't want your gifts. Please don't."

"Just do as I say, please Chrissie. It's no' much, really."

Chrissie closed her eyes and put out her hand and Tommy slipped the gold bracelet into it. She opened her eyes wide as she looked at the bracelet, before eyeing Tommy with narrowed eyes. "Where did you get this?"

"Same place I got this," he said, fingering his own chain.

"Is it legit?" she asked with a dubious expression.

"Aye, of course. It's for you, to show how much I care for you."

"How can you afford these, Tommy? I don't get it."

All his pent-up frustrations and anxieties began to surface, searching out a weakness or a crack in his armour, and it didn't take long before he lost control. "Is that your gratitude? Is it the best you can do?" Vaguely aware of the stares coming from the other tables, he lowered his voice. "Chrissie, what is it with you? Why do you pick these fights?"

"Tommy, where did you get these?"

"I bought them off a mate." Then to make sure of his point, he added, "I paid for them."

Chrissie slowly put it on her wrist and closed the clasp. "It's beautiful, thank you."

"Ach, aye. Can I get you a cuppa?"

"Please. Thanks."

He passed Andy back and went up to the counter, feeling pleased with how well things were going. He ordered the tea, paid, and carried the tray back to the table once it was ready.

"Tommy, I can't take this." Chrissie held out the bracelet.

Surprised, he put the tray down and reached across for Andy. "Why? What do you mean?"

The bracelet stayed in the palm of her hand. "I came today to tell you that I've been thinking about us and where we're heading. It's no good. It's over, Tommy. There won't be an 'us' anymore. You can still see Andy, I'll see to that. But I have to get on with my life. I want to be free to meet someone who'll love me in the way I need to be loved and who'll care for Andy like a son. I can't go back to how we were. You're just too unpredictable."

Nay, she can't do this to me!

It was as if two great continental plates had collided, sending tremors that shook his foundations, causing his hard crust to rupture. He gasped for air and pushed Andy towards her, scared of what he might do.

"I'm sorry, Tommy. I know this hurts, but it's for the best—for all of us. You'll move on and meet someone else, I know you will. Maybe she'll bring out the best in you. That's something I don't seem to be able to do." She fell silent, still holding the bracelet.

"Nay Chrissie, you can't. We need each other." One look at her set face and he knew it wouldn't work. Overcome by a rush of paralysing anxiety, he placed his head in his hands and flinched as pain shot through his cheek. Chrissie's bracelet hit the table beside him as the tears came freely. *What a mess I've made of my life. Da's right. I am useless.*

Time seemed frozen. Although aware of a gentle hand on his forearm, he didn't care any more. He just wanted to be away from here, to a place where he could be on his own, where it didn't hurt. Tea poured into the cups. Normal, and yet nothing was normal. How could Chrissie just carry on? Didn't she care?

She can go to hell, and so can all the rest!

The hand shook his arm and he lifted his sore head to look into her wide blue eyes. He wanted her to understand all his pent-up hurt, to hurt her like she'd hurt him. But she was still Chrissie and try as he might, he didn't hate her. Couldn't hate her. Perhaps it was his fault and she was an innocent party.

"Tommy, I'm truly sorry. How about a cup of tea?" Chrissie held a cup out towards him.

As if a cuppa will fix things! Not trusting himself to speak, he just stared at her.

As if to placate him further, she held out Andy and he took the bairn, holding him close as he struggled against him. They sipped their tea in tense silence.

"Tommy, I need to get going. Andy needs his nap."

He nodded and pressed a kiss onto Andy's cheek before passing him back to Chrissie. He watched her bustle about as she placed him in his pushchair and gathered her things. Her movements gave a sense of finality to it. *This is it, then.*

"Tommy, you can still see Andy. Call me." Chrissie started to move away, then turned and gave him a kiss on his cheek. A Judas kiss. She blushed and hurried out the door to the street.

Devastated, Tommy sat staring at the wall for he didn't know how long. The bracelet lay where she'd dropped it and he picked it up and fiddled with its links. Then with a heavy spirit, he slipped it into his pocket and left the tea rooms.

Instead of taking the tube back to the flat, Tommy walked. He didn't know where. He just kept walking as though searching for answers. It was hard to make sense of things and everything seemed to be plotted against him. His nose was in constant pain and kept bleeding, his head pounded. The nausea returned, increasing his misery.

Greater than the physical hurt was his guilt. Aye, he was guilty for hurting the New Zealand lass and guilty for hurting Chrissie. *How can I live with my mistakes?* And now he had to face John over the incident with the cabbie last night. How would he react? Would the cops come around? He was scared.

A couple of hours passed before he decided to head for the base. Perhaps being busy would distract him. He wasn't far from Golders Green and he decided to ride the bus the rest of the way. It was only a short wait at the bus stop and he jumped aboard, dropping coins onto the plate before moving down the aisle to a spare seat. His injuries attracted stares from other passengers and he hung his head. Five stops, and they pulled into a bus stop near the base where he left their stares behind, relieved.

Something was different about the base. The cabbies paused in their card game to stare at him. Then he realised that not only was there none of the usual uncouth banter, but the shelves were completely empty of the merchandise that had been there the night before.

"Oi, Jock, over here!" Dave called out to him.

Peeved at the continued use of the name, he walked over and said, "It's Tommy."

"I don't give a toss what it is. What the hell have you been playing at?"

"What do you mean?"

"You bloody well know what I mean. I took a call from the cops today. One of the black cab drivers has laid a formal complaint about you. Seems you were caught using their rank and you worked him over real good."

"That cabbie hauled me out of my cab and started to lay into me." His hand went to his cheek.

"You knew the rules and you broke them," Dave said in a tone that was more growl than speech.

"Aye and if you played fair, I wouldn't need to use their ranks. You give all the cushy jobs to those losers." Tommy gestured to the card players. "They spend less time on the road and yet they make more than the rest of us. How're we meant to make a crust?"

"Why, you bloody jock!" The vein in Dave's neck pulsed and his face was red with rage.

Something about the controller reminded him of his da' and it was too much for him. He took a step towards Dave and swung a punch. Dave spun in his chair and the punch missed its target. A hoot of laughter came from behind him.

"You realise what you've done? We don't need a bobby sniffing around this office. You've put us all at risk, you idiot!" Dave shouted.

"Aye, and you can stick your cabs."

"Get out!"

Tommy threw the keys on the desk and stormed out. It was still light outside, and he walked again, not caring where. He had lost everything—his flat, Chrissie, Andy, and now his job. He pulled out his fags and lit one before inhaling deeply, trying to find comfort. But the fag didn't replace the bitter loneliness and it provided little relief. His ma's kitchen flashed before him and he could almost smell the comforting aroma of her oat cakes baking. There was nothing here for him now. Perhaps he should just head for home and face the music. How much worse could it possibly be?

But for now, a night at the Jolly would help. He could do with Dobbo's sympathetic ear. It was time for a pint or three to take away the pain of the day's events.

*

Tommy opened his eyes and shielded them from the light as he tried to focus. His head pounded, and he pulled his jacket closer in an attempt to stop shivering. He was wedged between a row of rubbish bins and the wall of a building in a narrow cobbled alleyway. How had he got here? And what was that awful smell? His clothes were filthy, covered with blood and what looked like the contents of his stomach. That explained the smell.

Traffic droned nearby. Someone coughed, and Tommy turned. A tramp stirred in a doorway close by. Turning was a bad idea, as pain shot through his brain. He tried to get up, but slumped back down, dizzy and with his back and legs aching, and tried to recall the last few days since he'd seen Chrissie. Since the debacle at the cab office.

He'd found Dobbo in the Jolly Miller and he'd sat on a bar stool, telling him and any other punters who'd listen about his misfortunes over a series of pints. But then it got hazy. At some stage he'd been at the flat, arguing with Jerome while Dobbo acted as referee. He'd been drinking with a bunch of strangers at a party somewhere, but he had no clue how he'd got there.

His hand traced a path from his throbbing temples down to his nose. Pain triggered the memory of the run-in with the cabbie. He clutched his neck, but the gold chain was gone. A quick search of his pockets revealed they were empty as well. His fags, lighter, wallet, and keys were gone. And Chrissie's chain was gone. All gone.

He got to his feet slowly, gingerly, and reeled as the ground swayed under him. He leaned on the grimy wall to steady himself, then staggered out of the alley. The light hurt his eyes like shards of glass that pierced him. A drink would help numb the pain, but he had no money. And it seemed more important to get to the flat to sort things out. What time was it? When had he last eaten?

At the flat, he banged on the door. Footsteps sounded and Dobbo's face appeared at the door.

"Man, where have you been? I was worried about you." Dobbo eyed him up and down. "Good gawd man, you're a right mess. You'd better come in and get cleaned up."

"Ach aye, I woke out on the street—don't remember much. Have you anything I can take for this headache? It's a killer." He followed Dobbo inside.

"You'd better have a shower and change your clothes. I'll fix you something to eat—you must be famished."

After his shower, Tommy found Dobbo in the kitchen cooking sausages and eggs. The smell roused his appetite and he took the heaped plateful offered and dug in.

"Tommy, you know you can't stay here—especially after picking that fight with Jerome." Dobbo looked him in the eye. "Do you remember it?"

"Nay. I've only vague recollections of the last few days."

"You nearly slugged Jerome, and it wasn't his fault. You need to be out of here before he gets home from work—I promised him."

Tommy stopped eating and stared at his plate. Suddenly the food didn't taste all that grand and he picked at it with his fork. "Aye, I'll leave."

"Where will you go?"

"I don't know. Maybe I'll just head back home and face the music. There's nothing here for me now. There's no hope for Chrissie and me. And I've no job."

"Maybe that's best, to get yourself sorted out. What'll you do if the cops are looking for you up there?"

"Take off somewhere else, I guess. I'll work something out. If I need help, there's always Jimmy."

"Sorry, mate. I feel a right plonker having to ask you to leave. But maybe it's for the best. Maybe a fresh start up north will help you get over Chrissie."

"Nay, I'll never get over her." He tried to focus on the fork, but it wasn't working. His eyes brimmed and spilled over.

"Give her some time. She might change her mind."

"Nay, it's over this time."

They sat in strained silence.

"Ach Dobbo, I've had my pockets cleaned out, wallet and all—I don't suppose you could give me a wee loan?" He looked down at his plate. "I've nothing to repay you with. They've even taken the gold chains I picked up down the cab office."

"How much?"

Tommy looked up. "Would fifty quid and a pack of fags be okay?"

"I can't do fifty. I'll shell out for the bus ticket and give you a tenner for smokes and sandwiches. That's all I can manage. Sorry."

"Thanks. You've been a good mate."

"Now, how 'bout you pack up your stuff and I'll walk you to the tube station."

Although skint once more, a sense of relief replaced some of Tommy's anxiety. He'd soon be seeing Jimmy and Ma again. Perhaps things would start to look up.

13

Germany

It was mid-afternoon when the train pulled into Bremen, and Rose was thankful to have arrived at last. The moving tide of passengers jostled her as she stood on the platform, a lone pine on a hilltop being buffeted by a gale. Voices echoed around her, but she understood nothing. Fear hit, not for the first time since she'd left London.

She hefted on her backpack, and joined the tide turning towards the exit hall and made straight for the bank of telephones along one wall. But the instructions were in German, and she needed some local coins. She hurried across to the Bureau de Change kiosk, attended by a man whose face seemed to be imprinted with a permanent scowl.

"Kann ich Ihnen helfen?" he asked. She had no idea what that meant.

"Please can you change this into deutsche marks?"

He took the travellers cheques and counted out some notes and coins before slapping them on the counter with a receipt. "Der Nächste bitte."

"Excuse me. I need to make a local call on the telephone. Do I have the right change?"

"Nein. Weiter?"

Frustrated, Rose stuffed the money into her money belt and made her way back to the phone booth. A stout woman was leaving the next booth and Rose intercepted her. "English?" she asked.

"A little," the woman answered with a smile.

"Please, can you help me with the telephone? I can't read the instructions."

Rose slipped her backpack off and put it on the floor, standing over it with legs astride. It was the only way they could both fit in the small booth. Another time Rose might have found it hilarious, but right now she was too stressed. The woman explained how to work the phone and showed her what coins to use, before squeezing her way back out of the booth. Rose dialled the number and waited. It rang and rang and rang. After about twenty rings, Rose had to admit nobody was home. *What an idiot—I should've called her before leaving London. Now what?*

She hung up and retrieved her coins. The train departures were listed on a large screen, but it was confusing and she couldn't find one stopping at Berne.

She slumped onto a vacant bench seat near the phones and fossicked in her pack to retrieve her map from the side pocket. The scale was too small and of little use. Looking about, she resorted to her newly found strategy of positive self-talk to fight the panic that threatened to overwhelm her.

It's okay—I'm safe. Besides, this is the adventure I signed up for, and I know the chances of anything bad happening are infinitely small. I just need to get on with it!

As she looked around, she spotted an unmanned information kiosk in the centre of the complex. She humped her backpack over her shoulders and went to the desk.

Behind the array of maps and brochures was a large wall map that clearly showed the railway station. After searching virtually every grid she found Carmen's town, and compared it to her small-scale map, jotting down directions and highlighting the roads she'd need to follow. Relieved, she decided to refuel on bread and cheese.

She tried ringing Carmen again but was unsuccessful. There were no buses to Berne waiting at the bus stop. There were few options. She could either wait—and she didn't know when the next bus would come—or hitchhike. But she was filled with an uneasy tension—on one hand, she was scared for her safety, and on the other she needed to take a risk to overcome her fears. This trip was about facing fear and proving she was a survivor. Here was a chance to do just that, but could she?

Mustering her courage, she decided to hitch the forty kilometres from Bremen to Berne. She tucked her money belt under her shirt and gathered her things. With map and directions in hand, she left the station. *Let the adventure begin.*

Outside on the street, she paused as she tried to get her bearings. Somehow, she needed to get out of the city to a point where she could hitch. Another look at the map assured her that she needed to walk along the road to the river, cross the bridge and then look for the road to Berne. Once there, she should be able to start hitching. *But should I? Am I being foolish?*

She'd hitchhiked before, but never alone and never outside an English-speaking country. Maybe it was reckless, but she'd chosen to believe she was safer now that the odds were in her favour. She needed to do this, to conquer her fear. With this in mind, she mastered the last of her doubts and cautiously began her expedition.

It was good to be outside after being cooped up on the train, and she looked forward to getting into the country. The day was comfortably warm, although dark clouds were evident on the horizon. Keen to get to her destination, she walked with purpose, oblivious to the weight on her back. Everything around her was foreign and wonderful. The signs, the architecture, the shops. The people even dressed differently—and there wasn't a jandal in sight. The newness of everything was exciting and it tempered her angst.

After walking a couple of kilometres, she came to an intersection and checked her map. This road would take her towards Berne and she turned into it, relieved to leave the busy road. The cars drove at a more leisurely pace and the steady flow of traffic looked promising. The river was somewhere to her right, obscured by a thick row of bushes. On the other side was a neat row of identical houses, clad in red brick offset by dark slate roofing. Above, clouds were gathering and she groaned out loud at the thought of rain.

Fifty metres further, the road was wide enough for a car to pull over safely and it was time to find a ride. She stepped to the kerb, turned to face the oncoming traffic, plastered a false smile on her face, and put out her thumb.

A blue Citröen whizzed by without slowing. Undeterred, she smiled at the next car. A silver BMW passed without even a flicker. Continuing to hold out her thumb, she tried again. A lorry trundled towards her. It looked like he wasn't going to stop, but then he braked and pulled over onto the kerb. She ran forward to catch him. The cab seemed to loom over her and she was suddenly scared. *What on earth am I doing?* But she was committed to finding her way to Carmen's and wouldn't turn back now. She had to climb up onto the little step to reach the handle.

"Hello?" she asked, with a tremor in her voice, as she peered into the cab. "Um, speak English?"

"Nein, wo soll's denn hingehen?" The voice had a deep growl to it.

Oh no, he doesn't speak English. Now what?

"Berne?" She didn't even know if she was pronouncing it right.

"Ich versteh' dich nicht." Blonde and heavyset, his round face was scarred and marked with stubble.

She climbed into the cab and perched on the seat, her pack still on her back, ready to jump. Opening her map, she pointed to Carmen's road. "Berne?" she asked again.

He nodded and smiled to reveal the gap in his teeth. "Berne." It didn't sound anything like what she'd said, but he pointed to the spot on the map and repeated, "Berne."

This will be okay, nothing nasty will happen. She slipped her backpack off and put it on the seat between them.

He continued to smile at her, babbling something unintelligible. She tried to smile back, but her angst was too intense. Getting a grip on herself, she opened the map on her knee and resolved to follow their progress, to check they were heading in the right direction. Even so, she kept one hand on her pack and the other on the door handle, just in case she needed to make a hasty exit.

He moved the truck back into the traffic. She stole a glance at him and guessed he was in his mid-forties. A grubby orange tee shirt adorned with a picture of a bear and some words in Deutsch partly covered a pair of equally grubby shorts. His arms were muscular and hairy, his fingers stained yellow with black under the nails. He turned to look at her and she realised she'd been caught staring.

"**Was machst du hier? Warum willst du denn ausgerechnet nach Berne?**" He seemed to look her up and down.

Was he undressing her with his eyes? "Sorry, I don't understand. Only English." She gripped her pack and held the chrome door handle tightly in her right hand.

More unintelligible words, then he lapsed into silence.

The map lay open on her lap and she studied it, trying to see where they were. The truck began to slow and she looked up, searching for landmarks or road signs—anything to help check they were on the right track. A signpost loomed and she breathed an audible sigh of relief as she read the word *Berne*. The truck turned left and she found her place on the map. Now confident that they were heading in the right direction, her fear lessened but nevertheless she remained on guard. With her fear under control she could watch the countryside, the quaint houses with their orderly farmyards and the bright green of the rolling hills. Overhead, the clouds were looking more ominous.

They travelled on in silence for some twenty minutes before he spoke again, "Ich kann dich hier am Stadtrand absetzen. Von hier aus ist es nicht mehr weit."

"Sorry, nein Deutsch." She pronounced the words carefully.

Perhaps he appreciated her feeble attempt at his language, because he began to chatter again. The air brakes hissed as the great lorry began to slow before turning into a small side road.

Oh no, is this where it happens?

Panicked, she gripped the door handle as she weighed up jumping out onto the roadside. She could roll into the gutter and then make a run for the other road where a car would be sure to see her. The truck ground to a stop.

Again he smiled his toothless grin and reached over to take the map from her lap. *Now what?* He pointed to a spot on the map and chattered as he tapped it twice and then tapped on Carmen's road before pointing back up the road behind them.

She took the map from him and with overwhelming relief. She understood. He was dropping her off here, and it was only ten kilometres or so to Carmen's. His intentions were good. She folded the map and redeposited it in the day pack.

"Thank you. Um, **danke. Auf Wiedersehen.**"

"**Auf Wiedersehen und viel Glück,**" he said.

Opening the door, she scrambled down. Her pack bounced off the cab seat and bumped her on the head before dropping at her feet. She waved as he drove off, ecstatic to have passed the test, and feeling more bulletproof.

A red brick farmhouse with a steep thatched roof sat amid a vista of lush German farmland surrounded by mature trees. In the distance, a windmill slowly turned its arms. Chickens squawked and somewhere a dog barked.

She unfolded the map to check her bearings using the road signs. Confident of her location, she tugged on both her backpack and day pack before locating a new spot to hitch. This time she hummed a tune as she put out her thumb, her mood now so upbeat that even the threatening rain couldn't dampen it.

It wasn't long before a green Volkswagen Beetle drew up beside her, carrying an elderly woman with a gaudy scarf wrapped around her head.

Rose opened the passenger door, more sure of her pronunciation this time. "Hello, Berne?"

The woman smiled. "Ja." Then she said something more that was lost on Rose.

"Speak English?" Rose asked.

"Nein, Ich spreche nur Deutsch." The woman continued to smile and motioned with her hand for Rose to get in. "Komm, steig ein."

Rose deposited her backpack on the back seat and took a seat in the front. She got her map out and pointed to Carmen's address. The woman reached over and traced the road with a bony finger, the skin dry and cracked.

The car lurched forward as they found a gap in the traffic. Again Rose laid the map open on her lap, checking their progress. It was a more comfortable ride with this woman, who looked like a farmer in her gumboots and old-fashioned dress. Just as it was starting to rain, they pulled up outside a red brick house with a lichen-covered tiled slate roof.

"Hier ist es. Hier ist es." The woman spoke loudly, as if Rose was deaf.

"Danke." Rose opened her door to get out but the woman pulled on her arm. Alarm bells sounded as Rose paused, confused.

"Meine Banane," the woman said and held out the banana that had been sitting on the tray. "Nimm sie. Nimm

sie dir." The woman pushed it towards Rose, her smile lighting up her face.

Rose relaxed as she realised the woman only wanted to give her the banana. She could have kissed her.

"For me?" she asked, pointing to herself.

"Ja, ja", the woman replied.

Rose gratefully accepted the banana. "Danke." It was all she could say. She tucked the banana and the map into her day pack and retrieved her pack from the back seat. "**Auf Wiedersehen** and **danke.**"

Rain was teeming down as she waved the old woman off. With a last look at the retreating green beetle, she turned to face the twin doors in the middle of the two-storey building, their small verandas losing the battle to the protect them from the rain. Relieved to be here at last and anticipating a happy reunion, she hurried up the path and rapped the knocker.

Cowering close to the door to avoid the worst of the rain, she waited and her relief turned to dismay as the seconds drew out to minutes.

She knocked again, but there was still no answer. *Oh no, now what do I do?*

Again she knocked, louder this time.

Please Carmen, be home.

A window slid open above her to reveal a young man looking down at her.

"Ja?"

Desperate to be understood, she said, "Speak English?"

"Ja, a little." He was about her age, blonde although not particularly good looking.

"I'm here to visit Carmen. Do you know when she'll be home?"

"Nein, she goes to her sister's. Perhaps she gets home late."

Panicking, the familiar symptoms of her old anxiety returned—she prickled with hyper-sensitivity starting at the base of her neck, her breath came fast and shallow, and her skin became clammy. *Now what? Where should I go? What an idiot, why didn't I call from Brussels?* The rain ran down her face like tears and dripped off her chin.

"You not stay in the wet. You best come in here. I come down." He pulled the window shut and she heard footsteps on the stairs.

He was right, she couldn't just stand there in the rain. It might be hours before Carmen came home. But could this stranger be trusted? And what if Carmen didn't come home at all that evening? Her clothes were beginning to cling and her hair hung in lank wet strands. She had no choice but to accept his offer.

The door next to Carmen's opened and he stood there looking at her. "Come, please come."

With a thousand misgivings, she entered and heard the door shut behind her. She followed him up the narrow stairs and into a gloomy room, where the only light came from a small reading lamp over a kitchen table scattered with books and papers. A kitchenette was in a small alcove at the far side of the room and a bed was partially hidden behind a curtain. She shook as she lowered her pack to the floor near the top of the stairs.

"I, Oliver," he said in faltering English. He motioned towards an old wooden divan that was under the single window and adjacent to the bed.

"Hi, I'm Rose." What should she do? Did he want her to sit?

Muttering, he went out through an internal door beside the kitchenette, returning a moment later with an old towel, which he held out to her. She took it from him and dried her face and rubbed her hair dry, too scared to take her eyes off him.

Overladen shelves were bracketed onto one wall and he rifled through the muddle of books and papers before pulling out a pile of magazines, which he placed on the divan.

Understanding they were for her, she murmured, "Danke."

He shrugged and went across to the table and sat down. "I study." He glanced over his shoulder, then picked up his pen and shuffled the papers.

She put the damp towel down on the arm of the divan and sat on the edge of the drab upholstery. The bed was ominously close with the curtain no longer effective at this angle, exposing the rumpled sheets and scattered discarded clothes.

Her pulse pounded and she stole a look at him, but he appeared to be absorbed in his books. Determined to take control of her situation, she opened her day pack and rearranged the pepper pot and baton for easy retrieval. The old cuckoo clock on the wall ticked off the seconds as she waited. She opened a magazine. The letters were jumbled into unrecognisable words and she flipped through the pages, looking only at the pictures.

Time passed slowly.

Her sense of foreboding kept her on guard and she studied him over the magazine. The light illuminated his acne-scarred face, his long jawbone moving slightly as he chewed on a pencil. One hand played with the edge of a page in the book he was reading. His shoulder-length hair curled where it touched his scrawny shoulders. A faded burgundy tee shirt hung loosely over grey track pants. He didn't present a threatening picture, and he certainly didn't look like a psychopath—not that she had any idea what a psychopath should look like. The man on the track had looked innocent enough. Maybe they were wolves in sheep's clothing. Like this man? She dismissed the idea as absurd.

He stirred and turned; her eyes darted back to the magazine.

"I make soup. You want soup to have?" He appeared uneasy.

"No, thanks. I can wait for Carmen."

"It is no trouble. I make two soups." He got up and went into the kitchenette and busied himself with preparing the meal. She listened to him whistle as he worked. After a while, he came out and cleared a space on the table and set two places. "Come."

Rather than leave her valuables out of reach, she pulled her day pack over her shoulder and sat at the table. He'd produced rye bread, a large bowl of brown onion soup with grilled cheese on toast, and a glass of water. The delicious savoury smell aroused her appetite. For the first time, she smiled at this stranger who'd saved her from the rain.

"Danke, this looks wonderful."

"Please, sit and eat," he said, gesturing at her soup.

She picked up her spoon and poked at the cheese covered toast floating on top. It bobbed about on the steaming liquid. It was surreal, sitting here in this apartment having soup with this stranger. Self-conscious under his watchful eyes, she took a spoonful. The soup tasted so good that she became aware of just how famished she was.

"You like?" he asked.

"Yes, very much, thank you." They finished in silence, apart from the occasional slurps.

Comfortably full and with the threat now almost non-existent, she relaxed and chatted amicably with him in broken English. She learned he was studying engineering at a nearby university. He made them coffee and she shared where she'd come from and how she'd met Carmen. They were still chatting when a car pulled up outside.

Going to the window, he slid it open and called something out. "Come," he said, before scrambling down the stairs to open the door.

Rose picked up her things and hurried down the stairs after him. Carmen was standing just inside the door and Rose raced into her outstretched arms.

"So good to see you again," Rose said. "So very good."

"Rose, you come as a surprise. Why did you not call?" Carmen admonished her before laughing. "Come, I want to show you my home and we have so much to talk about."

Carmen and Oliver spoke in their native tongue before Carmen turned back to her. "We go now."

"Danke, Oliver." Rose followed Carmen out and into the apartment next door, overcome by a feeling of euphoria.

She'd conquered her fears and proven the worst was behind her. She'd put herself in difficult situations. She'd overcome. Her faith in human nature had been restored and there was an ever-expanding divide between her and that old abandoned railway line.

She lounged on the couch chatting happily with Carmen, filling her in on everything that had happened since they'd last met. The day couldn't have ended any better.

14

Scotland

Tommy paused at the white wooden door, turned the handle and stepped inside.

"Ma?" he called. "Ma, are you home?"

A chair grated across the floor in the kitchen. "My Tommy!" Ma emerged through the doorway, wiping her hands on her apron before stretching them out and enfolding him in her familiar bear hug. "Ach, you should have told me you were coming."

"Ma, it's good to be home."

She pulled away and looked at him. "Ach, what happened to yer face?"

"I got into a fight—it wasn't really my fault."

"Well, yer Da' won't be pleased. Come tell me about London. How's Chrissie and wee Andy? How long you here for? Are you just off the bus?" She paused to draw breath. "You must be tired and hungry."

"Ma—too many questions!" Tommy laughed, something he'd not done a lot of in recent times. It felt good. "And aye, I'm famished."

"Sit yourself down and tell me everything while I fix you something to eat."

"Where's Da?"

Her face clouded over. "Still at the school, but he'll be home soon enough."

As she busied herself at the bench, he looked about. Nothing had changed. A stack of magazines cluttered the table, and a stained cracked old mug of half-drunk tea sat beside them. The old Aga cooker with its yellowed enamel sat in its own enclave in the middle of the far wall, keeping the small room warm with its continuous oil burning. A drying rack was secured above it with a rope, the washing draped from its wooden slats. The sight of Da's shirts made him cringe, and he turned his attention back to Ma.

"It's over with Chrissie. She doesn't want me around, so wee Andy will grow up without his real Da'." He moved some of the clutter to make room on the old table. Its scratched wooden surface was familiar and it was comforting to be back there with Ma.

"I'm sorry, Tommy. Nay, that lass doesn't know what she's missing. I always thought you'd make a good da'." She came over with a pot of fresh tea and a plate of his favourite oatcakes.

"Ma, I lost my job cab driving and I'm skint—I was robbed. Dobbo loaned me enough to get home."

"Ach, Tommy, what next?" Her sad, tender eyes rested on him. "Best eat up and get your gear away upstairs before Da' gets in. Aye, you know how he hates a mess."

As if on cue the front door slammed and footsteps came up the hallway. "Tommy!"

Tommy stood up, his chair crashing to the floor. "Da'. I just got back."

"Aye, I can see that for myself." His deep voice seemed to fill the kitchen sending a shockwave of fear through Tommy. "What are you doing back here?"

"Chrissie and I are finished, so I thought I'd come home."

"She's finished with you, has she? What about the poor bairn growing up without his dad?"

"I can no' help it."

"Are you intending to get a job up here then?" The rant continued.

"Aye. Do you know of anything going?"

"And what skills do you have? What do you think you could do?" Da' gave him a dark look.

"I-I can l-labour or drive cabs."

"Cabs? In Lesmahagow? You're even more out of your mind than I thought."

"Ach, leave him be," Ma said. "He's only just walked in the door."

His dad turned on her, his large frame towering over her. "How dare you leap to his defence? It's because of you he's turned into such a failure."

Ma seemed to wilt. Tommy closed his eyes, trying to escape the tirade that he knew would come.

"If you stay here, you'll have to pay rent. And this time, I'll give you four weeks to find a job or else you're out. No more bludging."

Tommy opened his eyes to look at his Da' but made no comment.

"Do you hear me?" This time Da's volume had gone up a notch. The boiler was stoked and Tommy cringed, recognising Da' was on one of his rampages.

"Aye, I hear you."

"What happened to your face?"

"It was a misunderstanding with a Black Cab driver."

"You mean you still talk with your fists? Did you get the sack over it?"

"Nay—no' really."

"You're a poor excuse for a son, that's for sure. How did I get saddled with such a useless sod?"

"Please, Hamish, leave him be. He's only just home after a long trip." The words were spoken gently with a twinge of sadness.

"Woman, did I ask your opinion?" His hand clipped her across the side of the head and she whimpered as she recoiled, her hand touching her ear.

Tommy's first instinct was to cower, but his hatred for Da' was stronger.

"Leave Ma out of this!" Tommy could feel his eyes flashing with anger.

"Get out!" His da' spat the words out like venom.

Tommy picked up his chair, grabbed a fist of cupcakes, then shooting Ma an apologetic look he stormed out of the kitchen. In the hall, he picked up his things and hurried upstairs to his old room, slamming the door behind him.

Nothing had changed—his dad was still a bully. He lashed out at Ma so frequently it was almost normal. Tommy hated himself for not stopping the bastard beating her. Da' was cunning and would hit her where it didn't show, but Tommy knew how much went on. And yet, as petite as she was, Ma had always stood up for Tommy and more times than not she'd taken the punishment in his place. *Coward.*

He threw his bag into the corner and sank onto his wee bed. Dropping his head in his hands, he wept. *Why can't I stand up for Ma? Why can't I protect her like she deserves? Why do I just cringe when Da's around?* He pulled the faded blue cover with its bold thistle pattern around him, feeling like the small frightened boy that used to hide in this room. Ma had spent hours lovingly stitching the quilt and he'd always taken comfort from it.

The light outside was still bright, but not much made it through the small window into the north-facing room. The light that did make it through the drab net curtains reflected dully on the patterned wallpaper, matching his mood.

A small analogue clock on his bedside table showed six o'clock. Ma would be serving the meal. Da' liked routine and insisted dinner was dished up at the same time every night and Ma wouldn't disappoint. Tommy stayed in his bedroom. He wasn't hungry, and he preferred to avoid another confrontation. Da's words were ringing in his ears, filling him with self-doubt and recriminations. He'd lost it all—just when he thought he was finally making something of himself. To top it off he was a bully, no better than his dad, as well as a useless coward. *What's the point? What's there to live for?*

His pillow was wet. He'd been crying, and that only depressed him more. The tears challenged his masculinity, making him pitiful, but they wouldn't stop and he sobbed into his pillow.

What a mess he'd made of everything—the girl on the track, Chrissie and Andy, the cops, cab driving, Dobbo, his flatmates. Now he was back home, and he had nothing. *Is there anything left to look forward to?*

Jimmy. He'd go and find Jimmy.

*

The door opened and Jimmy's ma stood there. Seeing him, her lined face broke into a broad grin. "Ach, it's good to see you, lad. When did you get home?" She reached out to give him a warm hug.

"I'm just in from London. Is Jimmy about?"

"Aye, go on in. He's in the sitting room."

The door closed behind him and he made his way to the sitting room. This had always been his favourite place—somewhere calm where he could shelter from the fallout at home.

"Tommy, awrite?" Jimmy leapt off the sofa and slapped him on the shoulder.

"Aye, good to see you."

A movement behind Jimmy alerted Tommy to a pretty redhead, who now sidled up to Jimmy and slipped under his arm. "Tommy, meet my girl Nessie."

"Awrite, Nessie?"

"Hello Tommy, it's nice to meet you at last. I've heard so much about you." Nessie smiled shyly at him.

"You're a sly dog Jimmy Brown. You never told me about Nessie."

Jimmy laughed and said, "Aye, take a pew and I'll get us a brew."

He disappeared and Tommy sat in awkward silence with Nessie. This wasn't what he'd hoped for and he didn't feel like small talk.

"Jimmy says you've been in London," Nessie said.

"Aye, that I was."

"Are you home for long?"

"Depends." He watched her deflate and they lapsed into an uncomfortable silence. Soon Jimmy came bustling into the room with a couple of glasses and Mrs Brown in tow.

"When did you get back?" Jimmy's cheeks lit up in his trademark impish grin as he thrust him a glass of home brew. His red hair had grown and now curled around his ears, a striking match for Nessie.

"Cheers." Tommy raised his glass in a mock toast.

"Cheers to you, and good to see you."

"I came up on the bus today—I've been home and seen Ma."

"Have you eaten—can I fix you something?" Mrs Brown asked.

"Nay, thanks but I'm no' very hungry."

"I've a nice piece of Scottish Pie I can warm. You surely wouldn't turn down my pie?"

Mrs Brown had always been like his second ma and he'd polished off many meals in her kitchen. "Aye, that'd be grand, thanks."

Mrs Brown left the room, humming softly.

"So how's Chrissie?" Jimmy asked.

"Nay, it's over. She doesn't want us to be together. Andy's a real bonnie wee lad, though. You should see him."

"Ach, that's a shame. Still, she's no' the only lovely lass." Jimmy winked at Nessie, who smiled back.

Watching their interchange, Tommy pulled out a fag to cover his discomfort. Lighting it, he said, "I've been working as a cabbie, but I chucked it in. I think I'll stick around for a bit—there's nothing for me in London now."

"How did you get the bruiser?" Jimmy asked, then took a long sup.

"I was in a fight with a cabbie. It wasn't my fault, but in the end it cost me my job."

"Did you hear from the coppers?"

"Aye, I took a visit from one in London. No worries though." He didn't want to go into details in front of Nessie. "Did you?"

"Nay, nothing since you left."

Tommy gave Jimmy a questioning look and Jimmy turned to Nessie. "How about seeing if Ma needs a hand?"

"Sure can," Nessie disappeared out the door.

Once alone together, Jimmy asked, "So what did the cops say?"

"They visited Ma after I left, but she couldn't help them. They came to my flat in London and said they knew everything. Jimmy, the girl must've told them—she even knew my name. I reckon they're waiting for an opportunity to nab me. But Dobbo says they can't have enough on me, or they would've done it already. Maybe she's gone back to her own country."

"Cripes, are you sure you should be back here?"

"They found my flat in London, so I figured what's the difference? If they come after me here, I swear I'll disappear."

"And is there really no hope with Chrissie?"

"Nay, it's really over this time." Tommy hesitated. "What's with you and Nessie?"

"She's the best thing that's happened to me. I met her soon after you left and things developed. Ma loves her and she has Da' wrapped around her little finger. We decided she should move in here with me last week and so far it's been pretty darn good. She's a real special one. You'll see."

How could he expect Jimmy to cheer him up when he was preoccupied with a girl? It wouldn't be like the old days. Jimmy had let him down, and he skulled the rest of his beer in a silent act of defiance.

"Your pie's ready," Nessie said from the doorway.

"Aye, thanks."

They went through to the kitchen.

"Tommy, sit yourself down. You look like you could do with some home cooking." Mrs Brown placed a plate of steaming pie down on the small kitchen table where a place for one had been set. The aroma coming from his plate suddenly made him ravenous.

Something had changed. Gone was the old camaraderie that he'd always enjoyed with Jimmy. It was awkward. Their conversation stilted. As Jimmy flirted with Nessie, a pang of jealousy stung and Tommy felt alone.

*

"Tommy!"

Disoriented, he opened his eyes and struggled to adjust to the gloom. And then it came back to him—he was back in his bedroom in Lesmahagow.

"Tommy!" Ma called for a second time.

"What, Ma?" he called back.

His door opened. "I'm just off to the shops."

"Ach, aye."

"When are you getting up? Your da' doesn't like you staying in bed."

"I don't want to get up."

"Well, don't lie in too long. I'll be back by lunch." She closed the door and footsteps sounded on the stairs followed by the front door banging.

He curled up into a ball and wished he could disappear, leaving his worries behind. What was the use? His life was worthless. He was a bully like his dad, but Da' wasn't a coward or a failure. His da' would've stood the treatment in the Navy. Tommy hated who he was, what he'd become. Da' was right—he was a worthless excuse for a son. He wasn't a real man—he couldn't even protect his ma. Chrissie could see through him, and he wasn't fit to be a father to wee Andy. He had nothing and he was nobody.

The memory of the woman on the track filled his mind and he could see the fear in her eyes. He could almost smell her perfume. The power he'd felt had been hypnotic, but he hated himself for it. It hadn't been planned. It'd just happened. *How could I? Why? Why? Why?*

If only he could say sorry. He hadn't meant to hurt anyone.

Maybe the world would be better off without me. Chrissie won't miss me, and wee Andy will never know what he's missing. Jimmy looks happy enough with Nessie, so he'll no' miss me. Da' will be mighty pleased to be rid of the embarrassment his son has become. Ma? Aye, she'll miss me, but I'm no help to her. Maybe Da' would treat her better if I were gone.

Ma had always kept the medicines in the bathroom cupboard. Trance-like, he got out of bed and went through to the bathroom. A packet of aspirin sat enticingly on the top shelf of the cupboard. He opened it, finding there were plenty of pills.

The idea of a shower was appealing, so he stripped down and ran the water until it was warm. He stood for what seemed a long time as the water washed over him and ran down his skin. Like a ritual cleansing, it was somehow symbolic and spiritual. He turned off the shower and got out, moving slowly, each action deliberate. The worn towel was coarse against his skin.

Clad only in the towel, he headed for the bottle of Scotch that sat pride of place on the kitchen sideboard. There was a certain irony in taking his da's whisky. He filled a glass with the precious golden liquid, a glass that had been a favourite when he was a lad. These thoughts galvanised his actions. At last he was filled with purpose.

Back in his room, he took a piece of paper and pen from his old wooden school desk, covered in years of graffiti. He traced his finger along the etching where he'd carved his name one miserable day when rebelling against his da'. The significance of what he was doing hit him and his eyes betrayed him, tears flooding down his face. But he was defiant and with that came determination. Getting down on the floor, he began to compose a note.

Dear Ma,

There were no words to express what he wanted to say. Out of frustration he screwed up the paper and threw it into the corner. He took another piece and chewed thoughtfully on the pen. He wanted to say so much and yet there was really nothing to say, so he simply wrote:

Dear Ma,

I love you and I'm so sorry. Please tell Andy I love him.

Your son,

Tommy

He carefully folded the note and placed it on his pillow. The whisky tasted good. He took the aspirin, opened the foil blisters and emptied their contents onto the floor, placing them in a line. He began to swallow them, placing several in his mouth at a time and swilling them down with the fiery liquid. A fog seeped through his mind and reality faded.

Detached and yet somehow still conscious, it was like he wasn't there. Like he was hovering in the corner of the ceiling, watching himself. He could see himself lying on the floor. His body was still, the towel loose over his pasty skin. The whisky bottle lay on its side, its contents forming a dark shadow on the carpet. The empty aspirin packet lay amidst the broken foil blister packs. Was he dead? He didn't know.

He watched as the door opened and Ma rushed in. She dropped to her knees and hugged him to her, the towel no longer covering his nakedness. Her tears dripped onto his skin. Then darkness came.

*

Light shone through Tommy's eyelids causing him to stir. He groaned, tried to open his eyes, but the light was too strong. What had happened? Chasing the thought was like chasing a leaf in the wind while it danced and spun out of reach. Just as he thought he'd caught hold of it, it soared away again, teasing him. A soft warm hand was holding his and he forced his eyes open, blinking against the light.

"Tommy!" Ma's voice broke through the haze. She was sitting beside his bed, looking small and sad. "Tommy, I've been so worried."

"Sorry, Ma."

"You gave us a hell of a fright, lad." The deep voice was familiar and Da' was pacing on the other side of the bed inside a green curtain.

He was in a hospital room with sparse furniture and bare walls. Confused, he tried to get up, but the drip in his arm kept him down.

"Just rest, dear," Ma said with a quiet, gentle voice. "You're okay now."

He was alive. With closed eyes, he yielded to the drowsiness that engulfed him.

15

New Zealand, 1989

Rose sensed the presence of people, but a layer of deep fog separated them from her. It took effort to push her way through and open her eyes. Gary's face was nearby, his hand squeezing hers. Yet her eyelids were heavy, and she was sliding back into the dark place.

"Wake up, Mummy."

Lauren's sweet voice registered somewhere in her brain. With a struggle, her eyes flickered open. Lauren was close and her soft lips kissed Rose's cheek. Rose looked around the room and managed a weak smile. A nurse bustled about the bed, filling out her chart. Rose could remember her bed being wheeled to theatre and having to count backwards from ten. How far she'd counted, she had no idea.

"Rose, honey, we're all here. The kids and I have been waiting for you to wake up. You've done really well, and Mr Gurnsey says everything went to plan." Gary sat with Lauren and Michael, one on each knee.

"Did he? My arm?" Her throat was parched. "Can I have some water please?"

The officious looking nurse gave her a drink. "The operation was a success, and the surgeon will be around to see you soon."

"Thank heaven." Closing her eyes, she drifted on the edge of consciousness. Random and jumbled thoughts assaulted her, dark and frightening images. She forced herself to stay focused.

"Mummy, look at what they cut out of you." Lauren pointed to the bedside table.

A bone sat suspended in a jar of methylated spirits, complete with jagged flesh. "Yuck, gross!"

"Gurnsey dropped it off. He obviously used a hacksaw—it looks like the blade could've done with some sharpening," Gary said.

"What, as a trophy? What am I meant to do with it? Cook it?"

"Good to see you haven't lost your sense of humour," Gary said.

Footsteps came from behind the curtain, and Mr Gurnsey, dressed in a surgical gown and cap, appeared with the nurse.

"Good to see you're awake," Mr Gurnsey said. "Rose, you'll be pleased to know everything went extremely well. We had no trouble removing the rib—I thought you might like to see it and so I've left it in a jar for you."

"Ooh, that's grotesque. Take it away—I don't want a souvenir."

"Okay," he said, and laughed. "I found a lot of scar tissue in the cavity and cut it away as best I could. There was one piece that was a bit like a shoelace, and it was probably responsible for the symptoms you've had. The nerve was bundled up and I tried to untangle it a bit. Things should be better now. Any questions?"

"What do you think caused it?" Rose asked.

"I have no doubt the scar tissue resulted from a major trauma, most likely the assault you described."

She was vaguely aware Mr Gurnsey was continuing to discuss her recovery with Gary. A vision of the lonely path in Scotland came to mind and she was filled with fear. Instinctively, she recoiled and pushed back into her pillow, as if in self-defence, and winced with pain.

Mr Gurnsey's voice cut through her thoughts. "Easy, Rose. Don't try to move just yet. It's going to be painful to start with, and you need to take it slowly."

It was all because of that stranger. Angry, her tears flowed.

*

Rose walked through to the kitchen, where Gary was preparing dinner, careful not to jerk her arm. The forced inactivity while recuperating left her bored and edgy. A sudden movement shot pain through her ribcage causing her to wince, and she silently cursed her assailant. She sighed as she adjusted the sling holding her arm steady.

"Can I get you something?" Gary turned to reveal a worried expression that caused his moustache to droop even lower.

"Something for the pain would be good."

"It's only been two weeks and you're better every day. Not long now and you won't need these." He passed her the pills and a glass of water.

"I know—it's the sudden movements that get me. This pain keeps reminding me of the stuff I've been trying to forget—it took years to get over it and now it feels like it was just yesterday I was on that track. The emotional stuff is far harder to deal with than the physical. It's so unfair."

"I never expected it to have that effect on you. But you overcame it once and I know you can do it again. You've always been strong."

"It just makes me angry." She swallowed the pills and chased them down with the water. "I wonder how that girl's family is coping. You know, the one who was found strangled the night I went into hospital."

"The story went quiet. I suppose they're back in the UK now. I can't imagine what it'd be like to lose a child in that way—I hope we never find out."

"I can't believe the timing of it. It was so uncanny and it really messed me up that night before the op."

"The difference is this time you have me." Gary stepped forward and took her in his arms.

She allowed his strength to comfort and bolster her resolve. He was right—she'd done it once and she could do it again.

*

Six weeks had passed since her operation and now Rose was able to move without favouring her left side. Absorbing the jolts when riding in a car was no longer painful, so Gary had suggested a family picnic to celebrate her recovery. They'd packed a basket full of treats and headed for one of their favourite spots near a river.

Lauren chattered from her car seat in the back, feeding off their upbeat mood. Michael napped, oblivious to the excitement around him.

A track took them away from the road and down to a remote and empty car park, surrounded by lush native New Zealand bush. The shrill and vibrant chorus of the native birds was undeterred by their intrusion.

Lauren, in shorts and tee shirt, pulled on her small backpack, stuffed full of favourite toys. She looked cute with her hair in a French plait, a testimony to Rose's newly acquired use of her arm. Hand in hand, Rose and Lauren started off on the ten-minute walk to the picnic spot by the river, leaving Gary to follow with Michael and the picnic things.

Lauren prattled as they walked, and Rose offered vague responses. She was focused on the dense bush that surrounded the dirt track, and the dappled light that flickered through the trees and danced about the shadows. As they neared the river, the track widened into an open trail covered in grass and bordered with yellow flowering gorse. Her buoyant mood changed to one of deep foreboding, and panic threatened to overwhelm her as she was reminded of the remote railway track in Lesmahagow. Her pulse quickened, beads of moisture formed, and she shuddered.

She instinctively tightened her grip on Lauren's hand.

"What's wrong Mummy?" Lauren looked up with fearful eyes.

"Nothing. Sorry, Lauren," she said, trying to regain control. "Let's wait for Daddy and Michael to catch up."

With relief, she heard them long before they came into view. Michael's voice was loud enough to scare away any lingering ghosts. Her pulse slowed and the panic abated.

"You okay?" Gary asked.

"Sort of. I just had a moment, that's all."

"What do you mean?"

"A Lesmahagow moment, but let's not worry the kids."

Gary put down the hamper and drew her into him with his free arm. Lauren wrapped her arms around them both.

"Family cuddle," she said.

They resumed the walk, the silence broken only by the chatter of the children and the occasional birdsong.

On the riverbank, Gary set Michael down and laid out the rug on the bank. It was an idyllic setting for the picnic, with foxgloves providing a splash of vivid colour in the predominantly green landscape. Lauren pulled a small blue gingham tablecloth out of her pack and arranged a tea party with Little Ted, Jag the rag doll, and her little pink plastic teaset. Still feeling a little unnerved, Rose sat down on the rug with Michael and ferreted around the hamper crammed with goodies to find some snacks for the kids. Gary stretched out beside her. It was good to be out enjoying the sunshine.

"What happened back there?" he asked.

"I had a flashback—something about the path triggered a memory of that time in Lesmahagow. It scared me."

"Hey, we're on the other side of the world and you're safe now. I'll look after you."

"I know you will, but I can't help it. It just creeps up on me. I'd thought I was over it, but now it's constantly on my mind." She looked him in the eye. "Why can't I just bury it? Why do I have to go through it all again?"

"Just give it time."

"Aren't those foxgloves beautiful?" she asked, indicating a patch of bright flowers.

"Sure are."

She quietly contemplated them. "They stand so tall and bright, but they're hiding poison inside. Who would guess it just looking at them? Perhaps I've been like that. Maybe I've just done a good job of hiding my hurt instead of allowing it to be fully healed."

"I'm not sure something like this can ever be completely forgotten. Perhaps we're not meant to forget, for our own protection. You know, so we're smarter in the end."

"Well, I'd prefer to be smarter now."

"I don't like that your nightmares have returned." Gary poured the juice into a couple of glasses.

"I'm sorry I keep waking you up. I don't know how I can stop them."

"It's okay. You just need time. You got over them once, and you can do it again. I know you can. I'm just glad I'm here for you." He reached over and stroked her cheek with the back of his hand. "I can't remember when you last had one of those nightmares— before the op, that is."

"They seemed to peter out soon after we were married. But right now it just seems to take so much effort to remain positive. The lack of sleep is exhausting and I'm not sure I still have the fight in me."

"You have to believe you can get over it again. It's raw now because of the op."

"It's not just the op. It was also that poor girl who was murdered in the Bay of Plenty. That seemed so real. It could have been my story."

"But it wasn't. You're here and alive, and I'm here to protect you."

"I know that, and I know I'm not being logical, but I can't help it. You just need to bear with me for a while until

I can get myself sorted again." She forced a brave smile and lifted her glass. "Cheers. Here's to you—I couldn't do it without you."

It was true. Gary had been her rock ever since she'd returned from her travels. As planned, she'd arrived home in the November of 1981 and had found a job in the city where he was at university. Their relationship had continued to grow on the foundation built through their letters, and they married the following summer. The children had followed a few years down the track, and Gary had offered to be the house husband after a few disappointing experiences with childcare. It was a win for both of them as Gary loved nothing more than spending time with the children and she loved her work. In the early days of their reverse roles, she'd felt alienated by her mostly male colleagues. Some had the audacity to ask what sort of a man stays at home doing women's work. But now their arrangement was accepted. She'd been promised a promotion once she returned to work. Life was turning out better than she'd ever imagined.

Gary reached across for the hamper and pulled out the remaining food. They shared crackers with pâté and cheese while chatting about the kids and Rose's work opportunities. The peaceful babbling of the river washed over her and for a while Rose forgot the nagging and painful memories that plagued her.

A flash of colour caught her eye, and she turned to see Michael crawling towards the river. She moved to intercept him, but stopped and winced as sharp pain seared her shoulder. The pain brought fear and fear brought resentment and resentment stirred anger.

Gary had also scrambled to his feet to grab Michael and was now holding him and tickling him. Michael rewarded him with whoops of joy.

"You should have been watching him," she snapped.

"Excuse me?" He sounded hurt.

"Look, sorry, I'm just angry at my attacker."

"Rose, what can I do to help?" He lay back on his side, his head resting on his elbow. Michael sat beside him, snacking on a biscuit and content for now.

"Nothing. I'm angry that it ever happened." She lowered her voice so as not to alarm the kids. "I'm angry that when I think of Lesmahagow, I no longer think of Grandma and the place she grew up, but of the place I was attacked. Angry that I can't control my fears. Angry that I was over it, I had found my peace, but now that's gone. I don't want to live my life angry."

"And I don't want you to." His voice was quiet but strained.

She was silent for a moment. "Maybe you're right. I'm sorry for venting. I've forgiven him for what he did—I did that after the attack and maybe that's enough for me to move on. I don't think he could help it and I've always felt a bit sorry for him."

"That's one of the things I love about you—you've always been compassionate and you don't hold grudges."

"I try. There's a freedom that comes with forgiveness, for the forgiver as well as the forgiven."

"That's true. But it takes guts to forgive someone when they've really hurt you."

"But if I don't—if I harbour unforgiveness—then I'll become bitter inside and it will destroy me, like swallowing a parasite. It would eventually hollow me out, consume me. I don't want to be consumed with bitterness. If I was, how could I love you and the kids?" She handed Michael another biscuit. "No, I can't let it take hold of me."

He took her hand in his, gently playing with her fingers. "I'm glad you see that. I'm here for you, babe, whatever you need."

"Do you think I've truly forgiven him?"

"I think so, but it's hard to know." He paused and watched Lauren try to get Michael to join her tea party. "You can forgive the person and still hate what they did. My mum always said to separate out the actions from the person."

"I've often wondered what became of him."

"Perhaps it's best you don't know."

"I hope he never did it again to anyone else. Do you remember what one of the au pair girls in London said to me after it happened? She said that because I didn't press charges, if he did it again, I'd have to wear the guilt. If he'd gone on to murder someone, I'd be guilty of being an accomplice to murder."

"That's rubbish. You're not responsible for his actions—you have no control over what he does. You can't take that on your shoulders."

"Yes, but if I'd pressed charges, he'd have been out of circulation."

"It's probably unlikely he ever did do it again. Besides, you gave the police his details so they could check up on him, watch him, and get him help."

"I suppose so. But all the same, I'd like to know what happened to him."

"Perhaps you could do some research on, say, the serial killers in the UK at that time. You could look for copycat crimes."

"How would I do that?"

"You could ask at the library. They'd know."

"That's a brilliant idea—I'll do that. Thanks."

"I'll always be here for you. You know I love you and I always will." He reached over and kissed her, his lips lingering on hers.

"Ooh yuck!" said a small high voice, and they broke apart laughing.

The evening sun shone down and she soaked up its warmth, as though it had the power to burn away the snatches of memory that'd hounded her since the operation. Her confidence grew as she looked from Gary to Lauren and Michael, and she was determined not to let fear ruin her life.

*

Rose slowed as she turned the car into her driveway. Work had been frantic, yet she loved every minute of it. Her arm had healed after the surgery and she was back to full capability. The short distance between work and home was just enough to take off her professional hat and put on her family one, and now she couldn't wait to bath the kids and read them their bedtime stories.

Entering their small kitchen, she found Gary standing at the bench with Lauren standing beside him on a small plastic chair wearing her apron, and Michael playing at their feet with pot lids. She paused before speaking, absorbing the scene of domestic bliss.

"Mmmm, something smells good."

Gary turned to see her and his face lit up with a grin. "You're home early."

"I thought I'd surprise you and leave on time for a change. What's cooking?"

Lauren came running over and threw her arms around Rose. "We're making lasagne, Mummy. Do you want to help?"

Laughing, Rose answered, "No, I think there're enough cooks in this kitchen."

"A letter came for you—it's on the table," Gary said.

"Thanks." She scooped Michael up, kissed his chubby cheek and took him through to the dining room-lounge next door. She'd always liked this room, its character in keeping with the 1930's wooden New Zealand bungalow. The wood-panelled walls were enhanced by the rich glow from the evening light coming through the west-facing leadlight windows.

She picked up the envelope from the table. It was from the Hamilton Library. This was what she'd been waiting for, but she was afraid of what she'd find. She crossed to the far end of the room, to the ample lounge suite flanking the fireplace, and sank into the comfy green armchair with Michael on her lap.

After the picnic, she'd acted on Gary's suggestion to find out if there were any copycat crimes in Scotland or England around the time period she was attacked. She needed to be free from her guilt for not pressing charges, so she'd enlisted the library to help.

She stared at the envelope for a long moment. Was digging up the past a good thing? Or would it result in more guilt? She slowly opened the envelope and pulled out the letter, allowing Michael to take the discarded envelope. He climbed down and tottered back to the kitchen, his progress unsteady as he was still trying to master the art of walking.

Dear Mrs Cobham,

We are pleased to inform you that we have completed the requested search on crimes in Scotland and England between 1980 and the present, with the focus on assault and murder cases involving strangulation. Our contact in the UK has provided the following list of solved and unsolved cases.

Rose put the letter down. Did she really want to know if he'd hurt someone else? Perhaps completing the job this time? She read on. The names were unfamiliar and although she'd forgotten his name, she was sure she'd recognise it if she saw it. There were also very few in Scotland or involving Scottish criminals. One poor woman had been strangled in Edinburgh in 1983 and her body dumped in the river. Although the crime was unsolved, it appeared to be a one-off. She'd likely been right—her attacker had probably been an unfortunate and depressed man unaware of what he'd been doing. Intense relief replaced the guilt she'd carried for eight years.

Gary came over and sat on the arm of the chair and placed his arm around her. "Were they able to help?"

"Yes, and I feel so much better." She passed him the letter. "Here, take a read."

She waited for him to react.

"That's great, Rose. You can stop worrying now. Not pressing charges was the right thing to do, and we've a lot to thank that cop in Largs for."

"I think you're right. Waiting for a trial and having to go through the process would've been awful."

"I have an idea. What would you say to a trip back to Lesmahagow? Perhaps if you could visit the spot where it happened, you could put it to bed once and for all? I could come with you and it'd be like a pilgrimage. Do you think that might help?"

She looked up at him and saw he was serious and she loved him for it. "Gosh, I don't know—we have a mortgage to think about."

He gently stroked the back of her neck, and she flinched. She'd never gotten over the fear of being touched on the neck.

He withdrew his hand. "Sorry, I forgot."

"It's okay."

"But that's just it. You need to put this whole thing behind you once and for all." He took her hand and squeezed it. "Look, we could save up over the next year or two and make it a special holiday. Perhaps your parents could take the kids? I feel that if you could just face the place again, you'd see there's nothing to be afraid of anymore."

"Maybe it's not such a silly idea. A holiday overseas together would be fun and I'd love to show you some of the places I visited. You'd get the chance to meet my friends and family over there—they'd all love you." She squeezed his hand back. "Do you really think we could?"

"Sure, it'd be fun. Let's start saving for it."

"What if I see him in Lesmahagow?"

"What if you do? He can't hurt you now, not with me there."

The prospect of a pilgrimage back to the United Kingdom was both challenging and exciting. She could hardly wait to get the kids into bed so they could look at a savings plan. More than anything, she wanted to be free of her fears, no longer a slave to unwanted memories.

16

Scotland, 1991

Rose sat in the passenger seat of the rental car, bent over the map. "I think the next exit will be for Lesmahagow. Take the exit and turn right."

"Roger that," Gary said from the driver's seat. "How do you feel?"

"A little bit nervous, I guess. But I'll be glad to get out of the car."

"I'm looking forward to meeting the family."

"You'll love them. They're a sociable bunch." Staring out the window, she added, "I'm feeling a bit guilty that I didn't tell them the whole truth about my attacker."

"Rose, you can't worry about that. You did what you felt was right at the time. And from the way you told it, it was because you cared enough to want to protect them from taking the law into their own hands."

"But I still lied to them. Do you think I should I tell them now?"

"I wouldn't. It's been a long time, and what would you gain by changing your story?"

"Just a clear conscience."

"Well, my advice is to let it be. They probably don't want to rake over the details any more than you do."

"I suppose you're right, but I still feel guilty."

It was eighteen months since they'd started planning and saving for their trip and so far the British summer had exceeded expectations. After arriving at Heathrow, they'd spent a couple of hilarious nights with Stephanie and her English husband, John, and their daughter Lisa in their terrace house in Wimbledon. The years hadn't put any distance between her and Steph, and Gary and John had hit it off immediately. Yesterday, she and Gary had picked up the small rental car and headed for Lesmahagow, breaking the journey at a bed and breakfast in the Lake District. Rose loved sharing the experience with Gary, confident the kids were happy back home, being spoilt by her parents.

As they approached Lesmahagow, her tension increased and she wasn't sure if it was fuelled with the excitement of being here at last or by fear. The village looked better than she'd remembered it, brought to life by the sun reflecting brightly off the buildings. The boot shop was still advertising shoes and the church spire retained its commanding presence. They made their way up to Ted's place and parked outside.

Ted came rushing out of the house, grinning broadly. "Lass, it's good to see you back in Scotland." He stepped forward to hug her.

"Ted, it's great to be back at last—it's been a long time."

Inside, the kettle was whistling on the cooker and a comforting smell emanated from the oven.

"You must be parched after your drive. Put your things in the room opposite the bathroom and I'll make you a cuppa," Ted said.

Ted updated them with the family news over tea and biscuits at the kitchen table. It was as though she'd slipped back ten years, except Gary was beside her.

"I've organised a wee party for later this evening with the rest of the family. They're looking forward to seeing you. It's time we had another get-together." Ted turned to Gary and asked, "You a whisky drinker?"

"Afraid not. I've brought some beers."

Ted's face creased into a grin and his eyes twinkled. "Aye, a beer's okay, but before you leave here you'll be fond of a wee dram. I make my own whisky—I've a still out in the shed. I can show you if you like. I've experimented with a lot of different bases, but I'm most fond of carrot."

"Really—I thought bootlegging was illegal. How do you measure the strength?"

"Ach, I only make it for the family. I don't sell it, so I'm thinking no harm done. You can tell the strength by how many you can drink." Ted chuckled.

"Sounds dangerous. I might have to stick to the beer."

"We'll see. Now, is there anything in particular you'd like to do while you're here?"

"I'd like to show Gary the village, including Grandma's old place," Rose said. "And I'd like to take him up the track. You know, where I was attacked."

Ted's face registered alarm. "Nay, why dig up the past, lass? Going up there is not a good idea."

"I'd like to—it's something I need to face." She looked to Gary for support but received none.

"We tend not to talk about what happened. It was a shock to us all, and that's a fact."

It was a shock to them? Indignation rose as she considered it to be her trauma, she was the victim in this. Going up there was something she wanted to do, needed to do. No way would she be put off or have it ignored. "I had an operation eighteen months ago, and they removed the first rib on my left side." Her voice barely concealed her indignation.

"Ach, you poor child. And why would they do that?"

"There was old scar tissue interfering with the nerve and vein running down my arm, to the point I couldn't use it. The scar tissue was most likely caused by the attack."

"You don't say? I'm sorry to hear that. It was such a terrible thing. I've always felt guilty it happened while under my watch." He paused. "But some things are best left in the past."

It hurt to have her trauma dismissed in this way. "I'm sorry to bring it up, but I feel I need to see the place for my own sake." Her voice had an edge to it.

"Very well, you could go for a walk in the morning. The weather's looking good."

"That's great. I'm looking forward to seeing the village. Rose has told me lots about it." Gary gave Rose one of his looks that meant he understood.

"The folks will be arriving after dinner, and so we ought to have a quick bite to eat first."

Rose helped Ted serve the meal, and no more was said about the attack.

Cousins started arriving before the dishes were cleared and Rose introduced them all to Gary, who was treated like a long-lost cousin. Soon both the whisky and the Scot versus

Kiwi banter were flowing. Rose's heart filled with pride as she watched Gary.

There was a touch on her elbow and a soft voice said, "Rose, it's good to see you again." She turned to see Agnes and gave the older woman an affectionate hug.

"Agnes, I was hoping you'd be around tonight."

"Ach, I wouldn't have missed it. How've you been?"

"I'm good—we're fine, excited to be here."

"Aye, that's good. I've thought about you often. It was an awful thing that happened—I hope you don't mind me mentioning it," Agnes said quietly.

"No, that's okay. I guess I was just unlucky to be at the wrong place at the wrong time."

"We were all so sorry it happened, and here of all places."

"I wanted to thank you for your help—you were wonderful to me that day."

"Ach, I was glad to be there for you. Did you ever hear if they caught him?"

"No, I don't think they did. I did ask, years ago, before I left the UK. They hadn't then. I received compensation though, through the Victims of Violence scheme. They paid me three hundred and fifty quid, which bought me a car when I got home."

"I'm glad. I've often wondered how you'd coped—it must've taken some time to get over it."

"The physical injuries weren't too bad, but the nightmares lasted a long time. Then I had trouble with scar tissue in my thoracic cavity, and they had to remove a rib."

"Goodness, you poor lass. I hope that's the last of it for you now."

"Me too."

"We never speak of it. It was such a shocking thing."

"Ach, is it a private natter or can we join in?" Andy appeared at Rose's side, his arm around a pretty petite redhead with large green eyes.

"Of course, Andy. How are you? It's been ages." Rose reached out and kissed him on the cheek.

"Rose, meet Cilla, my wife." Cilla beamed and Rose liked her instantly.

"Pleased to meet you Cilla," Rose said, hugging her. They chattered with Agnes, and others drifted over to join in.

The small house filled with laughter and conversation, the noise level climbing as the drinks flowed. It was a good night. But no one else mentioned the event that had drawn these menfolk together in the same room ten years before. Then, it'd been a very different atmosphere. She was acutely aware that everyone in the room must have had it on their minds, and yet only Agnes mentioned it.

The omission felt awkward. While Rose didn't want to dwell on it, it was a real part of her story. It had to be on the minds of everyone in the room.

*

Rose spent a restless night in bed, the memories of her earlier visit haunting her into the small hours. Tired and unsettled, she was largely on autopilot during breakfast, her conversation strained. As the time for their walk neared, she became agitated and struggled to hide her rising turmoil.

When alone, Gary asked, "Rose, are you sure you're okay?"

It was one time too many for Rose. "For goodness sake, just leave me be." Gary immediately looked hurt and she added in a softer tone, "I'm sorry. I didn't mean that. I'm just a bit jittery."

Looking worried, he touched her arm, "Do you really want to go through with this?"

"Yes, I'm determined. The sooner the better, before I change my mind."

Taking their leave of Ted, Rose set a brisk pace for their walk down the hill and they only slowed down as they approached the corner with Langdykeside.

"Let's go up the hill first and get it over with," Rose said.

"Sure?"

"I need this." She hoped she sounded calmer than she felt.

He took her hand firmly in his and turned up Langdykeside. As they crossed the bridge, the sound of a loud engine disturbed the peace, making her uneasy.

"What's that noise?"

"It's okay. Just a posthole digger."

She said nothing, but her nervousness increased a notch. They followed the track up the hill to the old railway line. The sunlight warmed them, and Rose started to relax. She stripped off her sweater and tied it around her waist. They walked along in silence.

A man came towards them wearing faded jeans and an old tee shirt. Ill at ease, she edged closer to Gary. His hand gripped hers, reassuring her. But still she held her breath, not daring to take her eyes off the wiry stranger.

"Alright? Ach, it's a lovely day for it," the stranger said as he walked past.

"Morning," replied Gary.

She let out a long and quiet sigh.

Once the stranger was well past, Gary stopped and she looked up at him, still holding his hand. "Okay?"

"I guess so. Just another of those moments."

"You've got me with you this time." He brushed his thumb across her hand.

The ballast was rough underfoot and the long grass flicked at her bare legs. Her disquiet grew as the track opened out and they neared the spot. And then she recognised it. And froze.

Gary squeezed her hand. "Is this it?"

"I think so. It looks like the photo I took." She led him slowly over to the edge, her heart pounding. She could see through the bushes to the village in the valley below. "Just here."

She expected to feel fear rising within her, but there was nothing.

Gary placed an arm around her shoulders and drew her close.

Breathing deeply, her tension eased as she took in her surroundings. The hillside was vibrant with rich greenery that seemed lighter and prettier than she remembered. Heather bloomed with its delicate lilac flowers and the gorse was crowned in yellow. A grove of birches with their fine branches provided lace to the tapestry. The tall church spire rose majestically from the centre of the village. The warbling call of a skylark broke the silence and she watched as it rose vertically to a place so high that she lost sight of it, and yet its shrill song penetrated her soul long after it'd disappeared from view.

"Did you see that?" she asked.

"The bird?"

"It's a skylark. I feel like it was for me, a sign."

"How do you mean?"

"I'm not sure, but maybe it represents my freedom from this thing. Don't you think the skylark is special? Its flight is amazingly graceful and its song is so pure. It's not weighed down by anything—not fear or guilt or grudges. That's what I want."

"That's a bit deep."

She laughed. "Coming here has been good—I've no fear of this place. All I see is a lovely landscape. Nothing dark or sinister, nothing to fear."

Gary squeezed her shoulders.

"I've come a long way since that day," she said after a few minutes of mutual silence. "I've known what it's like to be lost to despair, but I've refused to let it define me. Even after the nightmares stopped, and for all the years since, I think the fear was always smouldering away just under the surface. Facing the op was enough to rekindle the fear, but it was much easier to overcome it this time around. And now being here, I know it's truly behind me."

Gary visibly relaxed his shoulders. "Thank goodness. I've been worried this might be a mistake. You know, coming back here."

"It's not a mistake. I feel I'm getting closure at last. What happened was an event at a particular time and place, but life moves on and this place has no hold over me." She turned to face him and he took her into his arms and held her as if she was the most cherished woman on earth.

"I'm free from its grip," she whispered. "I have no fear. I don't feel guilty over not pressing charges—and maybe lying to the cousins was necessary. And I do believe I've forgiven him. Although how can I be really sure?"

"If you don't feel any bitterness, then I guess you have."

"I don't think I do, but I don't know how to test it."

"You think too much—always the analyst." He kissed her long and tenderly, and any remaining tension dissipated.

"Now I think I'll remember this place for your kiss," she said as she pulled away.

"How about a memento of this beautiful place and the day I got closure?" She passed him the camera.

He snapped the photo, with the village nestled in the green hills providing a backdrop and the tall spire taking centre place beside Rose.

Hand in hand, they started back down the track.

"You know, I feel like a page has turned and at last we can start a new chapter," she said, her spirit light.

As they walked back down to the village, she related what she knew about Grandma's story. They paused outside the boot shop and she pointed out the rooms above. The old bell jangled as they entered the shop.

A little man wearing old-fashioned spectacles stood behind the counter. She recognised him and greeted him with a smile. "Hello Mr MacGregor. You may not remember me, but I visited here ten years ago. My great-grandfather used to own the boot shop. We're back on holiday from New Zealand and I was hoping to show my husband around."

"Ach aye, I do vaguely remember having a lass visit from New Zealand. You're a relation of Ted's, aren't you?" Mr MacGregor came around the counter towards them.

"Yes, that's right. I'm Rose, and this is my husband Gary."

Mr MacGregor shook his hand. "Welcome. I'm afraid there's no' much to see. The upstairs is no longer accessible from the shop—I've boarded it up. I've plans to renovate it and rent it out. Thought I'd make something useful out of the old place. Quite a few along the street have been done up recently."

"You don't mind if we just wander about?"

"Nay, of course not, lass."

The shop was much as she remembered it, with shelves laden with a variety of shoe styles and some modern posters adorning the walls. It just looked like any other shoe shop, with no obvious link to the past, other than the quaint welcoming bell.

Thanking Mr MacGregor, they exited and turned down the alleyway at the side of the building to take a look around the back. There they gazed up at the windows and Rose told Gary about the small decrepit rooms and how she'd imagined her grandmother's life had been.

"Who needs to look around upstairs when they've got you to describe it?"

Rose laughed. "C'mon, I'll show you the rest of the village."

As they turned into the street, a couple came towards them. They looked normal enough at first glance, but then a memory stirred.

Something about him was familiar.

As Rose stared, he stared back with his wide brown speckled eyes. And for a moment they were caught, frozen. Panic threatened but she forced herself to remain calm. *Was it him?*

<h1 style="text-align:center">17</h1>

They were out of milk. Tommy and Jeanie left their small flat on the edge of Lesmahagow and wandered down the main street towards the Co-op. Things had been looking up for him since he'd scored the job as a general maintenance lackey on the BP oil platform in the North Sea. His tour was fourteen days on followed by a fourteen day stretch at home and the pay was better than any he could achieve ashore. The real bonus to this lifestyle was the home leave every month.

He'd met Jeanie five years before and she was a tonic. Not one to suffer his mood swings, she'd been a stabilising influence and although his clinical depression was a constant struggle, the uppers prescribed by his doctor kept it under control. They'd been married a year and his life had become a continual cycle with Jeanie as the hub; rotating between time with her and time counting down until he'd be with her again. And now he had another event on the horizon—Jeanie was expecting and the bairn would be born in just ten weeks. Life had become more than just tolerable as the darkness that had hounded him was finally lifting.

"Penny for your thoughts?" Jeanie's words cut into his musing. "I'll wager it'll no' be a paintbrush." She giggled.

Their wee flat was in desperate need of a facelift. He'd promised to start with the bairn's room before his next tour, but the days just seemed to disappear. "Ach aye, a paintbrush. You need to pick your colours."

"I'm thinking something bright and cheery. Sky blue? Or yellow? Either would brighten up the room. I could get some fabric to make the curtains, maybe with teddy bears, something to bring out the wall colour ..."

He loved Jeanie's patience, her good humour and her lack of nagging. She was so easy to live with. Not like Chrissie, who'd had an unfortunate talent for winding him up. He hadn't seen her or Andy for years—not since she'd married the accountant from her dad's firm. Looking back, he realised he'd never stood a chance. They were young. He was stupid. It was clear now that he'd treated her badly. She hadn't deserved it. Just like Ma didn't deserve Da's temper. He wished he'd not hit her, for that he was sorry. But there was no going back. Jeanie was his girl.

"Are you listening to me?" Jeanie asked.

"Aye."

"So blue or yellow?"

"Ach, you choose. You know I'm no good at that sort of thing."

"Yellow then—not too bright and not too pale. Although it will depend on what I can find for the curtains. We should take a trip into Glasgow ..."

The counselling had helped him keep his anger in check. He'd learned to walk away rather than lash out. And he didn't ever want to hurt Jeanie. What they had was too precious. And soon he'd have his family.

A couple appeared out of the alleyway beside the shoe shop. They were dressed like tourists—shorts and tee shirts with flip flops on their feet. An old memory was revived somewhere in the depths of his brain. The tall, slim blue-eyed blonde stared at him as though frozen. Fear gripped him and adrenalin unleashed the all-too-familiar panic symptoms.

He stopped.

"Tommy?" Jeanie's voice sounded like it came from some great distance. He couldn't drag his eyes from the woman.

It was her. He was sure of it.

He'd never forgotten those penetrating blue eyes. A floodgate opened in his mind and memories tumbled through his consciousness, as if the dam holding back the loch had burst to expose the monster in its depths. He was back on the path, his hands around her throat, squeezing, wanting to strangle the life from her. He could see her eyes, pleading, willing him to stop.

Why had he done it? He didn't know. Perhaps because she was there and she was a woman. He'd been hurting and somehow by hurting her, he'd got back at Chrissie. But he couldn't blame a stranger for Chrissie's hurt.

He was guilty. Ten years of guilt reverberated inside his head. It had hung over him like a cloud and he'd learned to live with it. But now the protective shell he'd built up when getting his life together was crumbling, exposing his guilt—it couldn't be more obvious if it was tattooed all over his face.

"Tommy, what's the matter?" Jeanie tugged on his hand.

"It's you, isn't it?" The woman spoke with an antipodean accent.

"You!" The man at her side stepped forward, his face angry and fist clenched into a ball.

"No, wait." The woman put her hand on the man's arm and pulled him back.

Tommy couldn't pull his eyes from hers. Should he scarper? Cripes, could she still go to the police?

"It is you, I know it. It's your eyes. I could never forget them. You're the man I met on the track here ten years ago, aren't you?"

Sensing all eyes were on him, he could only stare, frozen as if caught red-handed.

"Don't go away. I want to talk to you." Her blue eyes pierced his.

"Tommy, who is it?" Jeanie quietly asked, close to his ear.

He couldn't speak. To admit he recognised her would be to admit his guilt. But he couldn't move either. He was caught. How could he keep it from Jeanie now?

"You were the one on the track." The woman spoke calmly yet firmly.

"Tommy, what's she saying?" Jeanie sounded frightened.

"C'mon Rose, let's go." The man spoke to the woman, but she didn't budge.

"No, I have something I want to say first." She turned to Jeanie. "I'm sorry, but there's something I've waited a long time to say to your friend. I don't want to make trouble for you, but can you just give me a few minutes?"

Jeanie nodded at the woman before turning to Tommy. She looked uncertain, but he nodded back, hoping to reassure her.

"Aye, you go on to the Co-op and I'll catch you up in a minute."

With a puzzled expression, she passed the couple and continued up the street, glancing back over her shoulder with a worried look.

The man remained silent, placing his arm protectively around the woman.

"You're the one that tried to strangle me—I recognise you."

"What do you want with me?" There was no way he was admitting he'd been the one.

"I want to say I forgive you. In fact, I think I forgave you soon after it happened." Her face looked strained.

Tommy stared at her. What was she saying?

She went on, as if gaining confidence. "Don't get me wrong. I hate what you did to me, what you put me through. It was hell and it's taken years to get over it." Her eyes had welled with tears, showing the depth of her feelings. "But I think it's important you know you're forgiven."

He could barely take in her words. The prisoner was set free. Tears spilled down his face. The pounding in his ears was his own rapid heartbeat. His throat tightened and he coughed. Guilt flooded through him. He hung his head, no longer able to look at her. "I'm s-sorry."

"There's something else. Ever since it happened, I've felt guilty because I didn't press charges. I need to know—and I need you to be honest—did you ever do it again?"

Surprised, he looked at her, tears dripping from his face, and she calmly held his gaze. "Nay, believe me never."

"Thank God." She was visibly relieved.

"Ach, I honest to gawd don't know what came over me that day. I'm so very sorry."

"I'm sorry too." She smiled at the man beside her, his arm still around her shoulder, and he guided her away, across the street.

Tommy stood rooted to the spot, watching them in disbelief. He took a hanky from his pocket and wiped his tears ... and was reminded of wiping blood from her neck. The memories he'd worked so hard to suppress were as vivid as if it'd just happened. It was surreal. Adrenaline flowed through his veins making him light-headed. He leaned up against the shop wall, took out his fags, pulled one out and lit up, taking solace in the thick smoke blanketing his lungs. Tears streamed down his face, but he didn't care.

She forgave him, even though he knew he didn't deserve it. It was as if a great heaviness had lifted.

He stood. He wiped his eyes. He laughed aloud.

He was free.

The cloud of guilt had hung over him for ten years and now he could move on. There would be no need to keep looking over his shoulder, wondering if it would catch up with him one day. He was free from it, even if he couldn't forget. He'd been given another chance.

But what if she'd been lying? No—she'd been earnest. Her face had shown how hard it was. And she could've kept walking—to avoid him—but she hadn't. She'd nothing to gain by lying.

He drew on his smoke while considering how much it must've cost her to say those words. It was gutsy and he wished he'd thanked her.

Jeanie came out of the Co-op, their bairn now a large bump, and he was filled with awe as he watched her come towards him. Her lush dark hair curled around her face and bounced on her shoulders as she walked. Even pregnant, her body was sensuous with the curves in all the right places. As she came closer, he saw the question in her wide dark eyes. Should he tell her? What would she do if she knew the truth? Would she forgive him? Would she still love him? Would he get to see his bairn? Or would she be like Chrissie?

He had so much at stake, and yet ... if the New Zealand woman could forgive him, he had to trust that Jeanie would do the same.

"What was that all about?" She sounded slightly out of breath.

"Ach, it's a long story. Let's get home and have that cuppa." He took the milk from her and held her by the hand, afraid she'd flee if he let it go. They walked in silence.

How much should he tell her? He was more scared of her reaction than he'd ever been of the cops. Yes, Jeanie was worth more to him than his freedom. He loved her. He couldn't afford to lose her.

Once home, they sat at the wee kitchen table and he watched her pour tea into a pair of mugs. She seemed tired. Should he burden her with this? Maintaining his secret had cast a long shadow that touched every part of his life and he'd been under it for a long time. He wanted to be free of it. Should he risk it?

"Tommy, you'd better tell me what this is all about." She reached her hand across to cover his.

"Ach, I don't know. I don't want to hurt us."

"You have to trust me, Tommy. I'm your wife, and I'm carrying your bairn." She looked him in the eye and held his gaze.

He looked away, not wanting her to see his guilt.

"Please, Tommy. Trust me."

"Aye, that I do. Jeanie, I did meet that lass—the one on the street today—around ten years ago."

"Was she a friend?"

"Nay, she was a stranger." He paused to draw in a deep breath. "It was when Chrissie had gone away and had my bairn and didn't want to see me. I guess I was desperate and depressed. I was on my way to the Post Office that day and something came over me. I don't remember exactly what happened or why, but I attacked that poor lass, up on the track above the village. I've no' seen her since—that is, until today."

Jeanie looked crestfallen and her hand pulled back from his as if it was poisonous. "Tommy, how could you do such a thing?"

"I don't know." He lowered his head as he faced his shame, silently pleading with her to give him another chance. Minutes seemed to pass as he waited for her response. Afraid, he lifted his head and looked at her.

"I'm so shocked," she whispered. Her normally good-humoured eyes overflowed with tears. "I just don't know what to say."

"I'm sorry. I truly wish I'd never been on the track that day." It was barely more than a whisper.

"How could you?" She scrambled to her feet, dropping the chair in her haste. "Tommy, how could you?" she shouted.

"Jeanie, wait—"

The door slammed behind her and footsteps stomped up the stairs. He slapped the table hard with his open palm—knocking his mug and spilling tea over the tablecloth. The outburst brought shame and he fought to control his anger. He lit a fag, to help calm his nerves. Now what? He couldn't afford to lose Jeanie. The house was quiet.

He waited. Finished his smoke. Ground the butt into the funny little Scotty dog ashtray, which reminded him of the day Jeanie brought it home as a present. He had to talk to her.

He went up to their room and stood outside the closed door.

"Jeanie?"

"Go away."

"Jeanie, please. Hear me out."

"What good will it do? I need to think."

He opened the door. Jeanie was lying curled up on their bed, eyes red and puffy, hugging her pillow. He sat beside her and took her hand, but she pulled it back.

"I'm so sorry I've let you down. But please, Jeanie, believe me when I say I'm no' that person—I don't know what came over me. It was a long time ago. It's never happened since and I promise it'll never happen again." His tension made his stomach clench.

"How can you promise that? What if you lose control with me, or worse, our bairn? Like your da' did?"

It was Chrissie in the teashop all over again and he couldn't let this end the same way. "I'm different now, and I've you beside me. I'm different with you. Better with you."

"I need to think, I'm going to Ma's. I don't know how long I'll be. I'll call you."

"Nay, Jeanie."

She got off the bed, pulled an overnight bag from the closet and grabbed a few items before leaving the house.

*

Two days had passed and Tommy was frantic. Not knowing was the worst, and he paced their small house like a caged animal. He hadn't slept well. The early hours were bleakest, when his mind would run riot with scenarios of how he'd lost Jeanie and his bairn.

He knew it was irrational, but he was angry at that woman for coming back—why did she have to jeopardise things now, when his life had been going so well with Jeanie? Then he'd find himself thinking of Andy and wondering what sort of a lad he'd become. Was he smart like his mother? Did he love footy like his da'?

It was almost time to leave for his next tour, and he had to sort things with Jeanie before then. Punishment for his stupidity all those years ago just kept on coming—and yet the woman had forgiven him. Why she had was something he'd never understand.

Now, if only Jeanie could forgive him.

A key in the latch interrupted his thoughts and his pulse quickened.

Jeanie entered the kitchen, her hand resting on her bulge. She looked exhausted. "We need to talk."

"Aye, we do. Sit down and I'll make us a cuppa."

She sat down and Tommy busied himself at the bench, filling the kettle, finding the mugs, getting the teabags.

All the while, Jeanie didn't speak. The silence was unbearable.

The kettle boiled, and he added the water to the mugs, his back to Jeanie.

"What did the woman on the street say to you?" Her voice wavered.

"That's what's so incredible. She said—." Tears welled up as the enormity of it hit him afresh. "She said she forgives me."

"Strewth! Forgives?" Her dark eyes were wide with surprise.

"Aye, I'm still trying to process it." Tommy came across with steaming mugs of tea and sat opposite her. "I'm sorry for my past. I never meant to disappoint you."

She stirred the sugar a little too long, before asking in a tone that betrayed her hurt, "Why hadn't you told me about what you did to this woman before? Didn't you trust me?"

"I was ashamed and guilty. And I didn't want to lose you."

"What other secrets are you keeping from me?"

"Nay, nothing. Please Jeanie, tell me we'll be okay. I've been scared stiff that if you'd known the truth you'd have left me." He looked her in the eye. "Please Jeanie, I know I don't deserve you, but I need you."

"I'm hurt, Tommy, hurt that you'd hide something like this from me. But I've been thinking." She paused and sipped from her mug. "I married you for better or for worse, because I love you. I can't pretend that I'm no' shocked and disappointed. Aye, I am that. But the man who did these things isn't the man I fell in love with." She took his hand and continued. "I know you're not a monster. I've seen the way your da' treats your ma and you're no' like that. I don't know what drove you to hurt that woman, but it's no' the Tommy Stewart I know."

Relief poured through him and he couldn't repress his smile. "You'll stay?"

"Aye, I'll stay. But no more secrets—promise?" Her eyes glistened with tears.

Tommy knelt beside her and took her in a tender but desperate embrace. Tears flowed.

He'd survived storms at sea with huge swells, but never one like the storm of guilt he'd been struggling against the past ten years. It'd surged and crashed over his decks. And now forgiveness calmed the storm and left him free. At that moment, he made a pact to never again lose his temper and risk losing Jeanie.

18

Rose allowed Gary to shepherd her down the street, away from the boot shop.

"Are you okay, Rose?" Gary asked once they were out of hearing of the couple, concern evident in his voice.

"Yeah, let's not go back yet. I don't feel like talking to anyone else."

"That's fine—we can just walk for a bit."

As they rounded the corner, the old parish church with its high spire and shiny brass clock came into view. "Let's go into the church." Maybe she'd find the solace she sought inside.

They walked silently through the gate into a churchyard inhabited by hundreds of years' worth of gravestones, many on a precarious lean. An imposing heavy wooden door creaked open at Gary's push, and they walked inside, their footsteps echoing on the stone floor. Her eyes soon adjusted to the gloom. The cathedral-like interior filled her with reverence and a deep sense of peace. Above her, she could see a large stained glass window depicting Christ descending from the cross. She sat on a hard wooden pew staring up at it, trying to make sense of everything that had happened.

"You were incredibly brave back there," Gary said.

"Not really. I didn't expect to see him after all these years and was surprised I recognised him."

Gary rested his hand on her knee. "I'm proud of you. But I wanted to smack him one. I'm angry for what he's put you through and frustrated I can't fix it for you."

"Thanks, but don't be angry." She paused to think, pensive. "I've been through that scenario many times in my head. You know, what I'd say to him if I ever met him. And I'm glad I've had the opportunity."

"Forgiveness is a powerful act."

"It sure is. I was never certain I'd forgiven him. I've said the words often enough, but had I actually forgiven him? It's hard to tell when you can't look someone in the eye. But now I'm positive. I can honestly say I had no bitterness when I met him just now."

"I guess that's always the ultimate test."

"I feel free from it all. I think that's what closure means."

"Did you believe him when he said he hadn't done it again?"

"I think he looked like he was telling the truth, and I want to believe it. I feel justified in not pressing charges. No more guilt. That's important. I never thought he should've been locked away."

"Locking people away isn't always the best answer, unless they're a danger to society. It's an expensive business."

"That's true—but I always thought he needed help. I'd love to know if he ever got any." She sat studying the stained glass picture for a while, thinking about the meaning behind it. "I wonder if he's truly remorseful."

"Seeing his reaction today, I'm guessing he is."

"Did you see his wife was pregnant?"

"It was hard to miss. How do you know she was his wife?"

"I saw a wedding band."

Smiling, he asked, "So now you're the detective?"

She chuckled. "Well, I'm glad he has a life. I hope that by forgiving him, he can also move on."

"That's fairly magnanimous of you." He laughed, slapping her gently on the knee, all tension gone. "You never cease to amaze me. I really do admire you, and I'm proud you're my wife."

"Well, I guess that day ten years ago was a dark day for us both. I have to believe he was mentally unstable at the time, and I can't hold it against him forever."

"I guess that's probably right."

"You know, each life is a story, and we're constantly colliding and bouncing off others, for good and for bad. These encounters can change the course of our lives, but we can control how we respond to them." She took his hand. "My story collided with a stranger's life back then and again today, but it's not my whole story. And he has no control over my life—not if I don't let him. I've learned that the hard way."

"You're right. You've been impacted by this experience and it's made you stronger. But you aren't defined by it—it's not who you are."

"In a strange way, forgiveness has disentangled my story from his. Perhaps now we are both free, no longer connected by fear and guilt."

"So now you're a philosopher as well as a detective?"

"I feel free and ready to move on." She laughed with him. "So perhaps now is the time to celebrate the end of a chapter."

Gary stood up and pulled her to her feet. "Let's just do that!"

ABOUT THE AUTHOR

Robyn Cotton grew up in South Taranaki and studied at Massey University, before embarking on her "O.E." to the UK. Settling back in NZ, she enjoyed a career in the dairy industry before becoming a management consultant and director. Inspired by her own experiences, she explored her interest in creative writing and launched her first novel *A Skylark Flies*. She followed up with her second book *Mary & Me*, also based on personal experience. Her third book *The Jibe* is her first mystery story.

She now enjoys life on the Hibiscus Coast where she can indulge her love of sailing while exploring the beautiful Hauraki Gulf.

Robyn is a Christian living with Parkinson's disease and likes nothing more than spending quality time with family and friends. Her other interests include photography, travel, various sports and exploring Aotearoa New Zealand's natural environment.

Mary & Me
Two women with Parkinson's disease two hundred years apart

By Robyn Cotton

Mary lives with Parkinson's disease in the early nineteenth century. Rose has it in the twenty-first century. Separated by two hundred years their experiences are vastly different, reflecting the change in attitudes and understanding.

Rose's story is inspired by the author's own experience of living with Parkinson's. It is deeply personal and honest and will take you on an emotional rollercoaster, from the shock of diagnosis to hope and resilience.

This journey illustrates the importance of responding positively to a life with a debilitating disease.

Mary & Me provides a novel approach to unpacking Parkinson's and the mix of emotions that may accompany it.

The Jibe

By Robyn Cotton

Ella Hampton makes a mayday call from Aurora on the Hauraki Gulf saying her husband has been lost overboard during a jibe manoeuvre. A body identified as Dean Hampton washes up with a gash to the head and other injuries. The coroner rules it an accident.

Amy Fagin, Dean's sister, while dealing with her recent diagnosis of young-onset Parkinson's disease, suspects something is amiss. Determined to find the truth about her brother's fate, she convinces Frank Smythe, of the Maritime Police Unit, to investigate the case further. Frank partners with Anahera Raupara to determine what really happened aboard Aurora.